PEACHES AND SCREAM

APPLE ORCHARD COZY MYSTERY BOOK 8

CHELSEA THOMAS

To Boris

For the milky toast, the tax help, and the memories.

Copyright & Disclaimer

Want updates, free cozies and recipes? Join the Chelsea Thomas Reader Club at chelseathomasauthor.com.

Cover Design: Priscilla Pantin

1

PEACHY KEEN

You know me by now, so you know that if I sit down to tell you a story, it's going to be about someone who died.

This particular story begins on a beautiful summer night, the first Saturday in August. That Saturday marked the official start of peach-picking season on the orchard. Miss May was throwing a huge peach party to celebrate, complete with fresh-picked peaches, homemade vanilla ice cream, and peach pie straight from the oven.

I'm not going to say I was only excited for the party because of the food, but the food was the most exciting part of the party... Yes, I lived on a farm that was primarily an apple orchard, but secretly, peaches were my favorite fruit. *Don't tell my aunt, Miss May!*

It had been a few months since the last murder in our small town of Pine Grove, and those few months had been beautiful. It had been nice to have a break from solving the crimes, even if deep down, I knew another mystery was on the horizon.

I'd enjoyed spending the long summer days in my

hometown — swimming in local watering holes, eating strawberry ice cream to cool down under the noon sun, and wandering the farm as the fireflies lit up the sky.

The orchard had a resident tiny horse, See-Saw, and in the past year we'd also acquired a limping little puppy dog named Steve and an orphaned cat named Kitty.

See-Saw, Steve, and Kitty were often my companions on my long walks. That was one of the many wonderful things about living in Pine Grove — there was never a shortage of good company, animal or human.

Summer was always a romantic season, and I'd spent most of that particular summer with my boyfriend, Germany Turtle.

Oh, Germany...let me tell you a little about Germany.

His parents had been murdered in Pine Grove, and I'd helped solve the mystery of their deaths. He was, *how should I say this*, a weirdo in a denim vest. Pretty cute, too.

That August night, as I walked across the orchard toward the event barn, my thoughts settled on Germany and my happy summer smile wavered. Before he'd moved to Pine Grove, Germany had been living in Africa and studying lions. The institute where he'd been doing his research had recently asked him to return, and he'd said yes.

It hadn't been an easy decision. Germany had insisted that he would stay home if I didn't want him to go, but I couldn't do that. Germany was supportive of me in all of my endeavors, and I wanted to offer him the same freedom and encouragement. I was sad to say good-bye to him, of course, but what could I do? Lions were his passion, and there were no lions in Pine Grove. At least not that I knew of.

When I entered the event barn, the smell of fresh-baked peach pie overwhelmed my senses. Sweet and tangy and buttery and delicious. Miss May had made at least twenty pies for the party and they were all lined up on a picnic table along the far wall.

Miss May set out plates along the table. She turned and smiled when she heard me enter.

"Chelsea. I take it from the look on your face that you're hungry for pie."

I chuckled. "I'm always hungry for pie. The look on my face is more about the beautiful summer night. The start of peach-picking season is so exciting."

"It really is," said Miss May. "A good way to bring in a little extra money, too."

I looked around, surveying the space.

I'd spent the prior day decorating the barn for the big peach extravaganza. In my former life as an interior designer living in New York City, I'd done a lot of upscale, modern design. But since moving back to Pine Grove, I'd gotten pretty good at the whole "rustic chic" aesthetic, *if I do say so myself.*

For the peach party, I'd arranged two long rows of picnic tables covered in classic red and white tablecloths (a go-to for rustic chic). A peach-shaped piñata dangled from the rafters, ready to be busted open by eager kids (and probably a few adults). A homemade sign reading, "Welcome to the Peach Party!" sparkled above the bandstand.

"Are Tom and the band going to be here soon to set up?" I asked.

I was referencing Tom, Pine Grove's erudite town lawyer. Normally a serious man, Tom loosened his proverbial tie as the frontman of his funky local band, *The Giggles.*

Miss May put another pie on the table. "Should be here any minute. Tom has been texting me about it all morning. He wanted to set up last night. He's so excited."

"Not a lot of gigs in Pine Grove," I said.

Miss May smiled. "You're right about that. So I suppose it makes sense. Do me a favor and set a pitcher of peach iced tea out on every table? I've got them all chilling in the fridge."

I clapped. "You made peach iced tea? Miss May, you are a goddess."

"I'm glad you finally realized that. Put out those red cups, too. People love drinking sweet tea out of red cups." I smiled and bounced over toward the large fridge, which we kept hidden behind a curtain.

As I crossed the room, I listened to the sounds of the evening. Crickets chirped their melancholy chorus out in the orchard. A gentle breeze lifted the edges of the tablecloths as it wafted through the barn. The thick perfume of wildflowers hung on the air. *Summer.* I felt it in my whole body.

When I was a little kid, coming to visit Miss May at the farm during the summer months had always been my favorite activity. I think my parents must have loved it too. I would splash in the creek and help bake pies and spend long nights laughing around a bonfire in the backyard. In the sepia haze of memory, those nights had the kind of perfection that only ever exists in the summers of youth.

After my parents died and Miss May took me in, I was grateful to have the *Thomas Family Fruit and Fir Farm* to call home. Even though I'd been devastated and numb after my parents' tragic passing, I'd found solace in the long aisles of the orchard and comfort in the natural sounds — the birds, the crickets, the katydids, the frogs...

I slipped out the back door of the barn, behind the bandstand, to take a moment to appreciate the quiet before the party began. Sliding my feet out of my sandals, I wriggled my toes in the grass. I closed my eyes for a few moments and focused on my other senses — the floral fragrance in the air, the damp warmth of the evening, the silky plushness of the earth beneath my feet...

My eyes snapped open when I heard footsteps rustling in the grass behind me.

"Chelsea. There you are, girl."

I turned back. Teeny approached me with an exasperated look on her face. "I've been looking all over for you."

Teeny was Miss May's best friend. Tiny in stature with an oversized personality, Teeny ran Pine Grove's coziest and most delicious restaurant, *Grandma's*.

"Sorry," I said. "I got distracted. I must have been out here for longer than I realized. It is such a beautiful—"

"Yeah, yeah. Beautiful night. Summer sounds. Perfect temperature. The peach pie smells amazing. We've got a situation in the barn, girl. May sent me out to find you."

My eyes widened. "Don't tell me—"

Teeny shook her head. "No. No one is dead. At least not yet."

I scratched my head. "What's going on?"

Teeny jerked her head back toward the barn. "Follow me. And you better high step it. It's a gorgeous night, but that doesn't mean the ticks aren't biting."

I took the highest steps I could as I followed Teeny back to the barn, her bleach blonde hair bobbing in the night.

Teeny was right, no one was dead...yet.

But murder was high stepping it straight toward us.

2

FIELD OF SCREAMS

I must've really been daydreaming out in the field for longer than I'd thought, because when I entered the barn, the party was in full swing. Tom Gigley and his band played "Millions of Peaches," by the Presidents of the United States of America. Twenty or so townspeople sashayed and swayed on the dance floor. And a little girl ate a big bowl of ice cream, chocolate sauce dripping down her chin.

I furrowed my brow. "It looks like the party is going fine. What are you so panicked about?"

Teeny didn't break stride. "Keep following. This is a classic *Jenna and Mr. Flowers* situation we've got our hands."

I cocked my head in confusion.

Teeny rolled her eyes. "You don't know *Jenna and Mr. Flowers*? It's my favorite new mystery show on the British mystery network. Jenna is a pet shop owner, but part of the pet shop is a cute little bookstore. And Mr. Flowers, well, obviously he owns a flower shop. The two of them never see eye to eye, but—"

"Teeny," I said.

She looked at me with her big, wide blue eyes. "Yeah?"

"The show sounds great but how about you tell me what's going on here?"

"I'm showing you. Patience is a virtue, young cricket."

"Grasshopper. It's young grasshopper."

Teeny scoffed. "That's obviously wrong. Grasshoppers aren't patient."

"I can't speak to the dispositions of the various insects, but I do know that the expression is grasshopper."

"Well in Britain, they say cricket."

Seconds later, Teeny led me out the main entrance of the event barn and we stumbled right into the problem. A large bald man and a short, squat woman were in the middle of a heated argument. I recognized the man. He was known around town as Big Jim. Big Jim owned a magic and illusion store on the outskirts of town and had always seemed like a nice guy to me. He was in his 50's and, like I said, as bald as a baseball pitched at a hundred mph.

I didn't recognize the woman with whom Big Jim was arguing. But she was red in the face. Wearing a long gauzy purple skirt and a rumpled, mismatched blouse. She had a ruddy face and stringy hair. The wild look in her eye gave me a sense of unease.

"You're a killer, Big Jim. You want to kill me. I know it. I can see inside your head, I can read the evil intentions scrawled on your little brain. Just admit that you want to kill me."

Jim laughed. "I told you already, Beth. I don't want to kill you. Why would I want to kill you? I'm a business leader in this town. I'm not about to give that up to kill someone I barely know."

Beth shook her head. "Barely know. You're acting like we don't have any history."

"We have history. I know that. But there's no beef between us now. Why would I want to kill you? We're cordial. We wave at each other from across the street. We make small talk in line the coffee shop."

I turned to Teeny. "This is bad. Where's Miss May?"

"Not sure," Teeny said. "I lost track of her whereabouts when I went to look for you. I don't know how to handle this dispute."

"Neither do I." My voice squeaked with nervous uncertainty. "I'm not the boss around here. It's not my job to stop these arguments. Sure, I've caught killers but I've never intervened in an argument about premeditated murder."

Big Jim must have heard me. He turned and took a step toward me. "Good. Chelsea. You're the manager here, right? Can you tell this woman to get off your property? She's losing her mind."

I stammered. "I'm sorry. Uh, let's talk this over. I understand the two of you are having a disagreement?"

"It's not a disagreement," Beth screeched. "This guy is trying to kill me."

I attempted my best reassuring smile. "I'm sure Big Jim is not trying to kill you. I don't believe we've met. I'm Chelsea. My aunt owns this orchard. You are—"

"I'm Beth. Just Beth. Don't call me Elizabeth."

"I wouldn't dream of it."

"I'm a tarot card reader. A medium. I know when people are up to evil. When there's a malicious spirit in the air I detect it and I attack it. That's what's happening here. If you're going to kick anyone off this orchard it should be that demon there." Beth pointed an angry finger at Big Jim.

Once again, he laughed. "This is preposterous." He zipped up his light summer jacket. "No need to kick me out, Chelsea. I'm leaving. I will be informing Miss May about how poorly you handled the situation. I've picked my apples here for twenty years. Today, I came hoping to get some peaches, but after this whole encounter... Not so sure I'll be back in the fall."

Jim took a step toward the parking lot. But Beth wasn't finished fighting. She stepped right in front of him and blocked his path. Her lips were pursed and angry. "Oh no, sir. You're not getting away like that. You are a killer. You need to be apprehended. If your crime goes unpunished now, there's no telling the evil that will the follow this community."

Big Jim mumbled. "We've already had like ten murders in the past year."

Beth took a wobbly stride toward Big Jim and got right in his face. "And you like that, don't you? I bet you had a hand in every single one of them. You're a despicable human. A horrible beast. I cannot let you leave this property!"

Beth lunged at Big Jim. I stepped between them with my hands held up to protect my face. "Wait! Hold on."

Beth froze. "What?"

"You say you do tarot readings, right?" I swallowed.

My change of subject seemed to calm Beth a bit. She stepped back and brushed off her hands on her skirt. She stepped back and composed herself. "Yes. I'm a medium. Magic is a skill that's been in my family for generations. I'm honored to continue it."

"That's so impressive," I said. "You must do so much valuable work. I appreciate that you're helping to keep our community safe."

"I'm not a threat to the community," said Big Jim.

Beth turned back to Big Jim with balled up fists.

"Hold on," I said, once again stepping into Beth's eye

line. “I have an idea.”

Beth turned to me. “Go on.”

“If there were real danger on my farm that would manifest itself in my energy, right? Do I understand that correctly?”

Beth nodded. “You grew up here, I’ve heard. Your aunt owns the place. You’re very involved in daily operations. Yes. I suspect if there were a presence of evil on this orchard your energy would reflect that. But I already know there is evil... I’m looking right at it.”

“I think maybe you and Big Jim got into a little bit of a tiff over nothing,” I said. “Maybe just take a break to cool down, Big Jim, you can check out the peaches. Beth... I would like for you to give me a tarot card reading. If my reading comes up clear, we’re all good and Jim probably isn’t trying to kill you. But if something is off, we can revisit this conversation with Jim. Big Jim, are you willing to hang out in the event barn while Beth gives me reading?”

“Is there peach pie left in there?”

Teeny stepped forward. “Plenty of peach pie. Not so sure about the ice cream, though. I had a few scoops. Maybe eight or nine. Who’s counting?! Once ice cream gets melty, I can eat it forever. I feel fine. I might have more.”

“Fine.” Big Jim turned to me. “I’ll be over by the pie.”

Big Jim trudged away. I looked back over at Beth. “This seems like a good plan to you?”

Beth looked at me with wide, panicked eyes. Like a deer in the headlights, but more frightened... like a deer who had just seen a ghost. When she spoke again her voice barely rose above a whisper. “I’ll be happy to give you a reading, Chelsea. But I must warn you, people aren’t always happy with what I have to say.”

I took a deep breath. “I understand. And I’m ready.”

3

READING RAINBOW

"I think we should do the reading in the bakeshop where it's quiet."

"Good," said Beth. "I need quiet to focus and channel the truth that is swimming in the universe. The truth loves to swim. When it swims it never drowns and its favorite stroke is the backwards crawl."

Teeny hurried to tag along. "That's pretty interesting stuff, Beth. You know what? I'm going to stay with Chelsea for this reading. Not because I don't trust you or anything like that. I just love the bakeshop. I love the way it smells and I'm gonna sneak myself a few chocolate chip cookies while we're in there. Who needs peach pie when you've got chocolate chip cookies? Is that alright? I'm sure it is. What were you saying about the backwards crawl?"

Beth crossed her arms. "I'd rather perform my reading one-on-one."

Teeny's eyes widened. "I understand that. But..." Teeny looked over at me for help.

"I have a lot of allergies," I said. "And Teeny knows what to do if I have an attack. So I need her by my side at all times. Especially if Miss May isn't around." I glanced back toward the event barn, then over at the farmhouse. "Where is Miss May, anyway?"

Teeny shrugged. "Not sure. Hope she's OK."

Beth held up a finger as though she were trying to detect the direction of the wind. Teeny and I stopped walking and exchanged a confused look. "Mabel Thomas is fine," Beth declared. "She is safe. I can guarantee that."

I bit my lower lip. "OK. Thanks for that information. I appreciate it." As we headed into the bakeshop, I felt a flush of worry redden my cheeks. *What was I getting myself into? Who was this Beth woman? Why hadn't I seen her before? Did she even live in Pine Grove?*

"I spend a great deal of time in Pine Grove. But I live two towns over. It's nice to be here for the Peach Festival."

Whoa.

How did Beth answer my question before I'd even said it? At first, I thought she'd read my mind. But I dismissed that thought. Coincidences often felt like magic. Not that I didn't believe in magic. Or coincidences. I just needed to keep my wits about me.

Teeny walked behind the counter and slid open the glass case, removing a few chocolate chip cookies. "I'm going to stand back here and test out this batch of cookies. You girls do your thing. Chelsea, if you're having an, uh, allergy attack like you do all the time, just grab your throat and gargle or say help or something. I've got the medicine."

I gulped. I didn't really have any severe allergies but at that moment I felt itchy, sweaty, and scared. *Perhaps I'm allergic to this situation*, I thought.

Moments later, Beth and I sat at a café table facing one another. Beth pulled a deck of tarot cards out of her purse and began shuffling them. She did not look up at me as she spoke. "Chelsea. Chelsea, Chelsea, Chelsea. Do you know how a tarot card reading works?"

I shook my head.

"First timer. That's fine. That's wonderful. Let's begin by setting our intentions for this reading. What do you want to know about yourself?"

"I'm not sure. I thought you planned to do a reading so we can find out if Big Jim wants to kill you."

Beth straightened the tarot cards on the table with a loud thud. She looked up at me. "Don't mention his name to me. That man is pure evil and his energy must not enter this room."

I stammered. "OK. Sorry."

"I can tell you are in love," said Beth. "But your significant other is far away right now. He feels a world away but you should know is always with you."

"Everyone knows Germany's in Africa," said Teeny from across the room. "Germany the person, not the country. Germany is Chelsea's boyfriend."

Beth glared at Teeny. Teeny covered her mouth. "Sorry. I'm being a blabber bottom. Sometimes I blab. Maybe you can hypnotize me later and we can take care of that bad habit — wham, bam, Bob's your uncle."

"I don't know any Bob," Beth said. I did my best not to laugh.

"Oh, 'Bob's your uncle' is just something they say in Britain," Teeny said with a dismissive wave.

"Well I'm not from Britain. And I'm also not a hypnotist," Beth said. She turned away from Teeny and looked me square in the eye. Her speech took on a lilting, distant tone. It felt as though she might fall asleep at any moment. Although her eyes were aimed at me they were unfocused and drowsy. "This reading, this reading is meant to bring you peace. What we find out we will find out. I've been doing this a long time, Chelsea. I know you, on a deep, soul-baring level...without us ever having met. That's the thing, with me. I try to know everything and keep myself informed."

I looked over at Teeny. I could tell from her face that she was also having trouble following Beth's logic. When I looked back at Beth, she snapped out of her trance and sat up straight. "I'm hungry. I need to eat before we do this."

I jumped to my feet. "Of course. Let me get you a cookie. Would you like a chocolate chip cookie?"

Beth swallowed with a loud swish in her mouth. "Yes. A cookie is what I need. My blood sugar can drop. I can't perform my duties here if my blood sugar drops."

I hurried behind the counter and grabbed a cookie off of Teeny's plate. "Chocolate chip cookie, coming right up. Would you like it warmed?"

Beth snapped at me. "I don't care about the temperature of the cookie. I said I need to eat. Now."

I hurried back over toward the table and placed the cookie down in front of Beth. She slipped back into her drowsy lilt. "I've never been a little woman. Some women, they don't need to eat. They're little birds. But I'm vibrant and strong. I need my sustenance and I'm not ashamed of that. I have no shame when it comes to fueling my body."

What are you supposed to say to something like that? I wasn't sure, but what I went with was, "Cookies are great. I love cookies. Yum. Hope you like it."

Beth took a bite and chewed in a slow and careful manner. Her eyes widened as she chewed and I could tell she liked the cookie. Our bakeshop had some of the best cookies east of the Mississippi. Probably west of it, too. But then, Beth tried to swallow and the cookie got caught in her throat. She grabbed her neck and coughed loudly. I slid my chair back.

"Are you OK?"

"Are you having an allergic reaction?" Teeny asked, in a panic.

Beth coughed for another moment. I hovered near her, unsure what action to take. "Can I get you water?" I asked. "Do you want me to do the Heimlich?"

Beth held up a hand to stop me. The coughing subsided and her eyes landed on mine with a cold, hard glare. She placed both hands down on the table and grimaced at me. When she spoke again her voice was steely and quiet. "I know you're trying to kill me, Chelsea."

"I'm sorry," I said. "I'm sorry about the cookie. Not... I'm not sorry for trying to kill you. I'm not trying to kill you. I'm sorry the cookie got stuck in your throat."

Beth balled up her fists. "You're trying to kill me. Just like everyone else. Everyone in this town wants me dead. I fled across the country in disguise. I thought I had escaped the federal agents. But they're after me. You are one of them. I told you, I already know everything about you!"

I stood up, knocking my chair backward. Teeny rushed toward me and pulled me away from Beth. "Calm down. Chelsea would never kill anyone. Karate chop, maybe, but kill, never! She's a sleuth. She catches killers. You're confused."

Beth stood. "I know who you are. You are the federal agents. You're the ones who want me dead."

The bakeshop door opened with a creak. "What's going on here?"

Miss May stepped inside, tall and confident, with her hands on her hips. "Beth. No one is trying to kill you."

"Miss May," I said. "Where were you?"

"One of our guests misplaced their cabin keys. I was looking out in the field. We'll talk about it later." Miss May took a step toward Beth. "Everything's OK, Beth."

"No, it's not." Beth's lip trembled. "Chelsea is a federal agent. She tricked me into giving her a reading so she could poison me with that cookie."

"Chelsea is not a federal agent," said Miss May. "She's my niece. I've known her my whole life. I've known you a long time, too. Remember? I used to come to your place sometimes? I'd bring fresh apples sometimes."

Miss May's relaxed and collected voice seemed to put Beth at ease. Beth unclenched her fists and let out a deep breath. "I like apples. And I like your orchard. It's important to have a connection with Mother Earth and the fruit that she bears."

"That's right," said Miss May. "But you know what? I need to close down the bakeshop to get ready for business tomorrow. This is been an eventful night. Why don't you head home and get some rest?"

Beth nodded. "Rest is good. Rest restores all."

Miss May held the door open and Beth crossed toward it. Just before Beth exited she turned back to me. "I know who you really are," she said.

"OK," I said. "Um… Have a good night."

Beth slammed the door as she left. The second she was gone, both Teeny and I breathed a big sigh of relief. "That woman is clinically insane," said Teeny. "And she had murder in her eyes."

4

MISS FORTUNE

After Beth vacated the premises I wanted nothing more than to discuss what had happened with Teeny, Miss May, and/or whatever animals happened to be around.

Yes, I talk to my animals. Yes, they talk back. It's a sacred bond, OK?

Anyway, I wanted to talk but I couldn't because we needed to do a lot of cleaning up after the peach party. I couldn't believe the mess that had been left behind in the event barn. Peach pie was smashed into the ground. A chair was knocked on its side. A big bowl of ice cream had melted on the bandstand.

All told, the cleanup effort took almost two hours. By the time Miss May and I finally made it back to the farmhouse for some much-needed rest, it was after midnight. We had discussed what had happened with Beth in passing as we cleaned, but the real conversation didn't start until we closed the door of the farmhouse behind us.

"Well," said Miss May. "That was an unbelievable night."

I laughed in spite of myself. "Unbelievable, yeah. That's

one word for it. I think I ate an entire peach pie all by myself as I was cleaning up. Do you think that's OK?"

Miss May laughed. "If you'd eaten any less, I'd be insulted. Those pies are good."

"Delicious," I agreed.

"Why don't you put on a pot of tea?" Miss May kicked off her shoes. "I'm going to change into my pajamas and sit by the fireplace for a few minutes before bed."

I nodded. "Decaf, right?"

Miss May gave me a look like, "obviously," then plodded up the creaky old farmhouse steps toward her room. I paused a moment to listen as each stair groaned under Miss May's heavy stride. The sound reminded me of being a teenager. Whenever I'd heard Miss May creaking her way up the steps, I'd known it was time to turn out my light, put my book away, and go to sleep. Funny how even a stern aunt approaching at bedtime can be part of a good memory.

I decided to make some of Miss May's fancy decaf chai tea that she kept in a jar above the kitchen sink. Neither she nor I typically drank much tea, but when we did we liked the good stuff.

I untwisted the jar and a bouquet of warm, savory spices drifted toward my nose. The tea in the jar was looseleaf, which meant it wasn't in a bag. It was just a bunch of leaves and spices mingled together in a fragrant heap.

I heaved a big spoon of chai into a pot and covered it with plenty of water. Waiting for the water to boil was agonizing. That expression about a watched pot felt particularly true on that night. Even more agonizing? Waiting for the tea to steep once the water had gotten hot.

After about ten minutes of waiting, I sifted the tea leaves into a strainer and I was left with a caramel brown liquid that made my nose tingle.

The next step in my tea recipe was top-secret, passed down to me from Miss May, *but I guess I'll tell you anyway*… I grabbed another jar and added a couple tablespoons of heavy whipping cream. Then I sealed the jar and shook it like a maraca for at least thirty seconds. Gradually, the heavy whipping cream got thicker and creamier — halfway between liquid and whipped. I stopped shaking the jar, added a touch of honey, then shook for another few seconds. Finally, I added the tea into the jar and gave it one more shake. Then I poured a big mug for both myself and Miss May and I took a big, indulgent sip.

The English way to drink tea was with hot milk, which was tasty, for sure. But I have to say, Miss May's recipe with heavy whipping cream was delicious. And, dare I say, better.

That first sip felt like falling back into a hotel bed. Soft and luxurious and warming, all the way through.

Miss May sidled into the kitchen wearing a nightgown covered with apples and I handed her the mug I'd poured for her. She took a sip and smiled. "We need to make chai more often."

I beamed. "You like it?"

"I love it. Oh! I know what we should do. We should make apple cider chai in the fall. Doesn't that sound delicious?"

"It sounds amazing."

"Remind me to remind you about that in a few months."

I chuckled. "Will do."

"For now, you need to tell me every detail of what happened with Beth in that bakeshop."

Miss May and I headed into the den. We sat by the empty fireplace, which was still cozy even in the summer, and I recounted all the details of the strange and unsettling encounter. The story shocked Miss May and I got a little sweaty retelling it.

Yeah, I've got the nervous sweats. I'm living with it. Thank you for your concern.

When I finally finished talking, Miss May shook her head. "I'm sorry you went through that. That poor woman, Beth... I don't think she's OK. Maybe I shouldn't have made her leave like that. She didn't even get any pie."

I put my hand on Miss May's arm. "You did the right thing. Trust me. But I understand. Everyone deserves a slice of that pie. Maybe we can bring her a slice in the morning?"

Miss May nodded. "I'll go to the door and you can stay in the car."

I grinned. "I wouldn't have it any other way."

Half an hour later, I tucked myself into bed with a warm, happy feeling in my stomach. But the longer I laid there, the worse I felt. My interaction with Beth had been tense and almost otherworldly. Nothing like I had ever experienced prior to that day. And the whole thing left me feeling uneasy, almost like Beth had cursed me.

The more I tried to push the thought out of my mind, the larger it grew. That's always how it seemed to work with me. After a few hours, I realized I hadn't slept for more than a few minutes. So I gave up on the idea of sleep and decided to work out my anxious energy with some middle-of-the-night baking. *What can I say?* Working in the bakeshop, I'd learned to stress-bake my troubles away. Baking was cheaper than therapy and more delicious too.

Down in the kitchen, I opened Miss May's baking cabinet and groaned with disappointment. We were almost out of flour. "Just my luck. I work in a bakeshop but I don't even have flour in my own kitchen."

I peeked out the window beside the front door and

looked out at the bakeshop. "I guess I could borrow some from out there."

My fussing in the kitchen had awakened Steve, our adorable little dog who walked with a serious (but still adorable) limp. Steve had been a gift from Germany Turtle. Ever since Germany had gone to Africa, Steve seemed to know that I needed a little extra affection. He wagged his tail and rolled over on his back, presenting his tummy for a quick rub. I patted Steve's belly and he whimpered. I couldn't be sure what his whimper meant, but it seemed to me like he was saying, "Yeah, Chels, you should definitely go out to the bakeshop to get some flour and make something delicious."

I gave Steve one more big pat, then straightened up. "Alright, Steve. You talked me into it. Let's go."

I grabbed Miss May's keys from the hook near the door and headed outside, Steve limping along excitedly beside me.

As I walked across the field toward the bakeshop, an ominous feeling overtook me. A full moon hung high in the sky. Fog draped over the apple trees, obscuring all but the lowest branches. And the night had gotten a little too chilly for my T-shirt and pajama pants.

My interaction with Beth played on loop in my mind as I approached the shop. I saw her wild eyes. I heard her strange muttering. I cringed when I remembered her choking on the chocolate chip cookie. *And accusing me of attempting to kill her...*

Steve started barking as soon as we reached the entrance to the bakeshop. "I know, buddy. We're here. Shhh."

Steve barked three or four more times, which was unwonted of him. I squatted beside him. "Hey. What's going on? Are you OK?"

Steve scratched at the front door to the bakeshop. "You want to go inside? It's cold. I know. Be patient."

I unlocked the door to the bakeshop, stepped inside and flicked on the light. There was Beth, propped up at a table with her deck of tarot cards laid out before her.

And she looked pretty dead.

5

MURDER, SHE PREDICTED

"Hello. Is anyone in here? I know karate." Maybe it wasn't the smartest move to try and talk to a potential murderer, but I wanted to make my presence (and my martial arts skills) known. Also, a tiny part of me hoped Beth would start awake, and turn out to be not dead at all.

I took a step into the bakeshop and scanned the room. Nothing seemed out of place. There were no signs of a struggle. But Beth didn't move an inch. Her wide, scary eyes didn't blink. A familiar feeling churned in my gut. It was the feeling I got whenever I discovered a dead body. And I'd discovered far too many dead bodies since moving back to Pine Grove.

I took another careful step into the room. A floorboard groaned beneath my feet. Steve barked at the sound. I stumbled back and put my hand to my chest. Then I took a deep breath and tried to steady myself. I'd been in this situation before, and I knew what to do...I needed to take a look around, sniff around for some clues, then call the police.

But I wasn't about to investigate alone. I pulled out my

phone and called Miss May. She answered with her groggy, sleepy, "why are you calling me right now?" voice.

"Sorry. I know it's late."

"It's fine." Miss May cleared her throat. "Is everything OK? What's the matter?"

"It's not good."

Miss May groaned. "Don't tell me..."

I sighed. "It's Beth. She's back in the bakeshop."

Miss May answered quickly. "What? She broke in?"

"I'm not sure how she got in. But she's dead."

Miss May whistled, low and long. "Don't touch anything. Be there in a minute."

Miss May ran to the bakeshop shortly thereafter and arrived more than a little out of breath. Her eyes were wide and panicked. "Have you checked to make sure the killer is not in here?"

I gulped. After calling Miss May, I had just stood perfectly still, like a scared little statue. Finding a dead body is shocking, no matter how many times you have the experience. "I wanted to wait for you to come. But I haven't heard anything. No one has attacked me. And when I asked if anyone else was in here, no one answered. I think we're alone." Steve barked. "Except for Steve," I corrected.

Over the next two or three minutes, Miss May and I conducted a careful search of the bakeshop. Looked behind the counters and under the tables and back in the storage closet. It turned out I was right. The killer was no longer in the building. He or she had escaped.

"OK. I guess we're safe. For the time being." Miss May sat on the stool. "Did you touch anything when you came in here?"

I shook my head. "Like I said. I was in shock. I still am in shock, I think."

"I know. Me too. We need to be observant. This isn't a typical crime scene. It's... staged."

I looked over at Beth, propped up and sitting before the tarot card spread. "I agree. This is odd."

"Tell me what you've noticed," said Miss May.

"Can you go first?" I asked. Miss May usually took the lead in our investigations, and I kind of preferred being her copilot.

Miss May shook her head. "You're a vital part of this investigation team. Tell me what you see and we'll analyze it together."

I looked around and put my hand to my chin. "First of all, the door was locked when I arrived. And all the windows are locked as well."

Miss May nodded. "Yes. No signs of forced entry."

"So the killer must have had a key to get inside and to lock up behind themselves when they left. But I have your keys. And my keys are back at the house. That doesn't make sense."

"I'll text KP and make sure his keys are with him." Miss May opened her phone and sent the text.

KP was the groundskeeper at the orchard. He was like an uncle to me — an uncle with a curmudgeonly exterior but a kind heart. I almost laughed out loud, thinking of KP getting a random text in the middle of the night. KP loved his beauty rest, as he called it. And he wasn't afraid to grumble when something made him unhappy.

Miss May's phone dinged with a reply from KP. I leaned forward. "What did he say?"

Miss May read the text. "He said, 'Do you know what time it is? I can't stay gorgeous if you text me in the middle of my slumber. I was having a good dream, too. I had all the pizza in the world and I never got full or gained weight.'"

I chuckled. Miss May shook her head. "I wish he'd answer the question about the keys."

Miss May's phone dinged once more. "It's another text from KP," she said, opening her phone. "'I've got my keys right here. You should know that because I've never lost anything in my entire life. Nighty-night.' Alright, that answers that."

Miss May showed me the phone. There was a picture of KP holding up his keys with a scowl on his face.

"Is there anything else missing in the bakeshop?" Miss May asked.

I nodded. "When we locked up there were three peach pies left in the display case. Now there's only two."

"That's right," Miss May said. "So technically two crimes have been committed here tonight. Murder and burglary. Although I'm not too upset about the loss of a single pie."

I looked over at Beth. Rigid and lifelike, her palms down on the table in front of her. "I want to say I'm surprised by this — and I suppose in some ways I am. Murder is always surprising. But Beth seemed convinced someone wanted to kill her."

"She seemed convinced everyone wanted to kill her." Miss May climbed off the stool and crossed toward Beth. "Including you, Chelsea."

I shuddered at the thought. "Beth made a lot of enemies, even just in the past few hours. She yelled at half the people at the peach party."

"She was hostile and paranoid," Miss May conceded. "And you're right... She had plenty of enemies."

Miss May snapped a photo of the tarot cards spread out on the table in front of Beth. "You don't know how to read these cards, do you?"

"No." I crossed over toward Miss May and took a look at

the tarot cards. There was a skeleton man rowing a boat. There was a knight trudging into the distance carrying a sack of swords. And there was a skeleton riding a horse with the word DEATH scrawled ominously beneath it. “These images freak me out,” I said.

Miss May nodded. “Everything about this crime scene freaks me out. The locked door. The missing pie. The tarot cards.”

I scratched my leg. “Maybe...it’s possible... Could Beth have died of natural causes? I don’t see any evidence that she had been in a fight or resisted.”

Miss May shrugged. “It’s possible. But I think she was poisoned. By our peach pie.”

I gasped. “Our peach pie isn’t poisonous! What makes you say that?”

Miss May pointed at a few crumbs on the table beside the tarot cards. “She definitely ate a slice before she died. Either that, or she was forced.”

I backed away from the table. Miss May was right. There were crumbs on the floor by Beth’s feet as well. I’d recognize those buttery flakes anywhere. The last thing that Beth had ever eaten was a slice of our peach pie.

Soft sunlight seeped into the bakeshop through the front windows. “Sun’s coming up.”

Miss May walked over to me and put her arm around my shoulder. “Come on. We need to call the cops.”

6

COPS AND PIE ROBBERS

Detective Wayne Hudson was tall, broad, and *fine*, also handsome. His piercing green-blue eyes were hard to look away from, even if the conversation you were having with him was awkward or weird. And Wayne and I had plenty of awkward conversations.

Yes, sometimes my chats with Wayne had a romantic undertone, but a lot of them also had a murderous undertone. Since I'd gotten together with Germany, Wayne had kept his distance. Part of me wondered if Wayne was still interested in dating me — and an even smaller part of me hoped he was.

The morning that Miss May and I found Beth dead in the bakeshop, Wayne was the first to arrive on the scene. He pulled up in an unmarked car and although it was barely dawn, he wore a neat brown suit that looked like a custom fit.

Is it bad that I noticed the fit of his suit right after having found a dead body?

I couldn't help myself. It was a good suit. Brown went

well with Wayne's green-blue eyes. Then again, Wayne looked good in pretty much any color.

OK. OK. Maybe I was noticing Wayne a little more than usual. Germany had been gone for a while at that point. Maybe I was a little excited to have an interaction with a single male. Even if the circumstances were bleak.

I stepped out of the bakeshop and met Wayne halfway down the walk. I gave him a small smile but his face was serious. "Hi Wayne. Sorry to call you out here so early."

Wayne pulled out his little detective notebook without looking at me. "Not a problem. Here to do my job. Can you describe the scene of the crime? And tell me why you were out in the bakeshop in the middle of the night? You know the drill."

"Yeah. Of course I know the drill." I leaned over to try and get a better look at Wayne's face. He resisted looking at me. I felt an anxious lump right in the center of my throat. I was embarrassed about my momentary feelings toward Wayne...he seemed to be in a purely professional mode.

Miss May and I had solved more murders than the Pine Grove Police Department by that point. Wayne had helped, sure. But the killers would've never been caught if it hadn't been for me and my aunt and Teeny too, sort of.

I took my time describing the scene of the crime. From prior experience, I knew I had to be careful with my words. I didn't want to incriminate myself nor did I want to end up a suspect in this investigation. I'd learned many times that Wayne and the other members of the police force in Pine Grove subscribed to the belief that the person who finds the body is often the guilty culprit.

I had discovered more than my fair share of bodies since moving back to Pine Grove, and I had never been the guilty culprit. But I didn't trust the police and I really, really didn't want to end up in jail for a crime I had not committed.

After I finished with my story, Wayne asked me to bring him to the bakeshop so he could string up police tape and look for clues. At that point, Chief Flanagan, Deputy Hercules and a few others had arrived on the scene. So after I let Wayne into the bakeshop, they crowded inside and asked me to exit.

I passed the next half hour or so sitting on the steps of the bakeshop beside Miss May. We were both tired and neither of us said much. I trusted Miss May's brain wheels were turning or churning or doing whatever they did. I felt too tired to start solving the mystery. I knew that this moment might be our last little bit of peace and quiet until we caught the killer, so I tried to relish the silence.

Wayne's boots clacked as he stepped out of the bakeshop. "You ladies say there are only three sets of keys to this establishment?"

Miss May nodded. "That's right."

Wayne walked toward us. "Care to show me those keys?"

Miss May dangled her keys at Wayne. "Mine are here." She unlocked her phone to show Wayne the picture of KP from earlier in the night. "These are KP's."

Wayne turned to me. "Chelsea. You have keys of your own?"

"Yeah. They're back in my room at the farmhouse."

Wayne just stood there. I looked over at Miss May and she shrugged. Wayne cleared his throat.

"You need to see them?" I asked.

"That would be nice."

I let out a deep breath and stood. "Alright. Let's go."

We trudged slowly back toward the farmhouse. The journey, which had only taken Miss May thirty seconds in her panic earlier that night, took us closer to two minutes. We didn't speak much as we walked. Then we got to the farmhouse and went inside.

"I know exactly where they are," I said. "In the left pocket of my jean jacket."

Wayne nodded. "I'll stay down in the foyer with Miss May. Bring the keys down when you find them."

I plodded up the stairs and into my bedroom. *I'll be honest, the place was a mess*. But I knew exactly where I'd left my jean jacket. On my chair, under three dresses, next to a pile of old diaries, between the window and my collection of books that I one day intended to read.

I grabbed the jacket and reached into the left pocket. The keys were not in there. *Weird*. I reached into the right pocket. No keys. I began to sweat.

I spun around, looking at my messy room. Then, the search began. I threw clothes left, right and backwards, listening for the jangle of keys as I excavated. I got on my hands and knees and looked under the bed. I accidentally knocked the chair over as I crawled under my desk.

Normally, I was very good at finding things. I had a proven search method, and I almost never came up empty-handed. But a combination of stress, fatigue, and feeling like I'd been cursed by a dead woman had me off of my game.

"You OK in here?"

I turned. Wayne and Miss May stood in the doorway to my bedroom.

"Um..."

"Your bedroom's a mess," said Wayne. *How observant, Detective.*

"It's not usually like this. I've been packing. Yeah. I've been packing for a trip to Morocco. I'm going there to learn how to make Moroccan rice. We're going to start serving Moroccan rice in the bakeshop."

Wayne crossed his arms. "You can't find the keys, can you?"

I gave Wayne a tiny shake of the head, at most one millimeter left and one millimeter right.

"And you said the door to the bakeshop was locked when you arrived?"

I nodded, again with the slightest movements.

"And the door can only be locked using a key?"

Another tiny nod. Half a millimeter up, half a millimeter down.

Miss May stepped forward. "You think the killer stole Chelsea's keys and use them to infiltrate the bakeshop?"

Wayne nodded. "That's right. And as long as the potential killer is out there with those keys, it's not safe for either of you to remain on this orchard."

7

THE KEY TO HAPPINESS

KP arrived at the farmhouse about ten minutes after the detectives left. He stepped through the front door and dragged his heavy work boots clean with a sigh.

Miss May threw up her hands in confusion. "Where have you been? I texted, I called."

KP shrugged. "You woke me up about the keys and I sent you a picture. Then I went back to sleep and apparently all this kerfuffle went down. I woke up in the middle of my sleep cycle before — when that happens and I go back down, I go back down hard."

"The cops were knocking on your cabin door for five minutes straight. They want to question you."

"Like I said. I go down hard. Hard as an uncooked bean at the family reunion. I just broke a tooth biting into one of those beans." KP groaned as he sat at the kitchen table. "Someone mind giving me all the details? You girls know I love the gossip."

Miss May and I exchanged a nervous glance. KP let out a long, slow whistle. "Don't tell me we've got another corpse on the farm. I just got my peaches fresh and juicy for picking. This is going to ruin business."

Miss May crossed her arms. "KP." She stood and sounded like an angry Catholic school teacher.

KP held up a hand in apology. "I know, I know. May the victim rest in peach, I mean peace. Rest In Peace. I got peaches on the mind, what can I say? Who was it, anyway?"

Miss May set a cup of coffee down in front of KP then sat across the kitchen table. He sipped his coffee in silence as she told him every detail of what had occurred in the bakeshop. When she was finally done speaking, KP didn't move or utter a single syllable for almost a full minute. Finally, he looked up. "What in the world is a tarot card?"

Miss May shook her head. "That's your question? You hear that entire story and you want to know what a tarot card is?"

"Hey. I'm not the detective. I'm just a curious farmer who had his sleep disrupted. Forgive me if I'm not quite as sharp as I might typically be." KP crossed to the counter and poured himself some more coffee. "You two want to be topped off?"

I nodded. There was plenty of adrenaline in my system from all the excitement of the prior night, but I suspected that I was in for a long day, or even a long week. Extra coffee was always essential in times like those. That, and extra sugar. "I like my coffee—"

KP sighed, cutting me off. "I know. Lots of sugar. Lots of cream. Barely any coffee."

"I'll have mine black," said Miss May. "To start, at least. Cream and sugar for dessert."

KP scoffed. "You two girls don't think I know how you like your coffee yet?"

Miss May grinned. "Our sleep was interrupted last night. Forgive us if we're not as sharp as we typically might be."

KP put our coffee down on the table and plopped back into his seat. "So you say the cops suggested you vacate the premises? Just because of some missing keys?"

I sipped my coffee. "That's right. Like Wayne said, that key ring had a key to the house, not just the keys to the bakeshop."

"So Wayne thinks this killer is going to come back, unlock the door to the farmhouse and kill the both of you girls for no apparent reason?" KP sipped his coffee.

"He doesn't think it's safe," said Miss May. "And I agree." Miss May put her hand on my arm. "I think we should go stay at Teeny's while we investigate this murder. No need to put ourselves in more danger than we already do in our detective work."

KP laughed. "You two are something. May, do you really think this killer stole Chelsea's keys? The girl loses her keys three times a day. Loses her phone every twenty minutes. One day last week I saw her on the farm only wearing one shoe. Lost the left one."

"That last part is true. I really don't know what happened to that shoe." I picked at the chip on my coffee mug. "I see your point. I can be forgetful. But I almost always find things!"

KP threw up his hands. "I'm not judging you for it. Most brilliant people are erratic, and you're the smartest girl I know. I'm just saying, keep that in mind. Don't go run and hide when the keys are probably under your bed somewhere."

I bit my lower lip. "You have a point. Although I looked everywhere I thought they might be."

"And we'll keep looking," said Miss May. "As time allows.

We need to move forward with this investigation and I don't think looking for Chelsea's keys is the best way to do so. If the killer has the keys, finding the killer will lead us to the keys. If the keys are lost in the house, they'll turn up sooner or later once we're moved back in."

I nodded. "That makes sense. But... What if the killer stole my keys and planned to use them to frame me for this murder? I mean... Beth already accused me of trying to kill her in a public place. Might be the beginning of a strong case against me."

"I thought of that. That's exactly why we need to get started on this case. Now."

I turned to KP. "Are you going to come stay at Teeny's with us?"

KP waved me away. "I'll be in my cabin. Like a guard dog. Not like Steve, he's a terrible guard dog. Too friendly. That's another reason for me to stick around, somebody's gotta feed Steve. And that tiny little pony See-Saw. And that new cat you two dragged home." KP had a point. The farm did require upkeep, but still, I didn't want him to risk his life.

"Are you sure you don't want to come, KP?" Miss May asked. "It may not be safe here."

"Like I said. I'm a guard dog. I'll hold down the fort. You girls stay safe and find this killer."

8

TEENY TOWN

Teeny lived in a cute two-bedroom craftsman just outside the center of town. Her house was a soft shade of lavender. It had bright white, Victorian-style trim and a big porch with three enormous rocking chairs. Teeny was sitting in the middle rocking chair when we pulled into the driveway. But she jumped up to meet us before we could get halfway to the porch. "Finally. I've been waiting all morning."

Teeny tried to pull the suitcase from Miss May's hands. "Give me that. You're a guest in my flat."

"This isn't a flat," I said.

"'Flat' is what they call a house in Britain," Teeny snipped.

"Nope," I muttered under my breath, but Teeny was too distracted trying to steal Miss May's bag to noticed my rebuttal.

"You're not carrying bags into the house," insisted Teeny.

Miss May yanked the bag back. "It's heavy, Teeny. Probably weighs twice what you do."

"So what? I'm strong. You don't think I'm strong? Don't

call me tiny." I laughed. Teeny spun on me. "Don't you laugh at me. I could bench press you like it's nothing."

Miss May shrugged. "OK. You can take my bag."

Miss May let go. Teeny immediately drooped under the weight of the luggage. She took two small steps, then dropped the bag. "What do you have in this thing? Bricks? Frying pans?! I have frying pans, May. They're perfectly good."

"You want me to carry it?" I offered.

"No," said Teeny. She began dragging the luggage toward the front door. Teeny sighed and wiped her brow as she led us into the foyer of her adorable home. The place was perfectly decorated and immaculately clean. It always had been spotless and I had a feeling it always would be. There was an overstuffed couch facing the fireplace. There were a couple of comfy armchairs. And there was old-fashioned art depicting Pine Grove from long ago on the walls. Teeny's house had always been one of my favorites in town and I was excited to stay there.

Teeny turned to us with her trademark wide smile. "Come on. I'll give you a tour."

Miss May hung her head. "Teeny. We've been here hundreds of times."

"So what? I got some new stuff. I want to show you. And I did up your room and everything."

Both Miss May and I knew there was no point putting up a fight so we joined Teeny on the tour. She showed us a nice painting of a pine tree that she had bought from a local artist the prior week. She showed us where she had stocked all her favorite foods in the kitchen. She showed us where all the extra toilet paper was, that was actually helpful. And she took us to our room. It was bright pink with two double beds and a fresh bottle of water on the nightstand.

"What do you think?" Teeny asked.

"I think it's very nice," said Miss May.

Teeny shook her head. "I don't care what you think. I want to know what Chelsea thinks. She's the interior designer."

"This is beautiful, Teeny. I've always loved your house. Thank you for having us."

"Are you kidding? This is a dream come true for me. I've always thought the three of us should be roommates. Like a version of *The Golden Girls* where they're all young."

Miss May laughed. "This really is nice, Teeny. Thank you." "

"Stop thanking me. Start solving this mystery." Teeny walked out of the bedroom and led us into the kitchen, where fresh baked cookies were on a big plate. "Sit. Talk."

We all grabbed a cookie and sat around the table.

"Let's start with suspects," said Teeny. "Who could have done this?"

"According to Beth, everyone wanted her dead," I said. "So a list of suspects might be kind of long."

"I don't think we should start with the suspects," said Miss May. "I think we should start with trying to understand more about Beth."

Teeny pointed at Miss May. "Smart. Very smart. I love that. Now take a bite of cookie. I want to know what you think."

My eyes widened. "I already ate two cookies. They were amazing. Chocolate chip goodness. How do you make them so gooey on the inside?"

Teeny raised her eyebrows. "That's a secret I've been perfecting for years. If you want to know you're going to have to kill me."

"Not in the mood for that kind of humor right now, Teeny." Miss May said.

"Fine. I take them out about two minutes early and let them set. By the time they cool, they don't taste underdone, they're just gooey and delicious. There's my secret. And you still haven't told what you think of the cookies, May."

"They're great, Teeny. You know I think they're great because I sell them in my bakeshop."

Teeny scrunched up her mouth. "Oh yeah. Forgot about that. So what do we know about Beth?"

"This one's a little tough because she lived a couple towns over," said Miss May. "Beth has been around for years and years and she was in Pine Grove often, but somehow it's different when someone is not a resident."

Teeny took a bite of cookie. "We know she was strange."

"This may be a rumor," said Miss May. "But I heard she was only recently released from *Five Pines.*"

I coughed up a bit of cookie. "*Five Pines* the mental hospital?"

"That's right."

"I suppose it's not too shocking," I said. "She seemed like she struggled with paranoia. And maybe a little schizophrenia or something. I mean, she was suspicious of everyone."

"What else do we know about her?" Teeny asked.

I turned to Miss May. "Did she have any genuine expertise in tarot cards? Is that something she's being doing for a long time?"

Miss May's jaw dropped. "Great question, Chelsea. I think you know who we need to talk to first."

Teeny jumped her feet. "Who?"

Miss May grabbed her car keys off the table. "I'll show you."

9

SALAZAR SPEAKS

Salazar was Pine Grove's only licensed, accredited psychic. I wasn't sure what kind of license he had, but I did know he had one from somewhere.

He lived in a little fairytale home nestled deep in the forest outside of town. Miss May and I had visited him on prior investigations, and he had been helpful, if eccentric. So when we started up the hill toward Salazar's house, I realized exactly where we were headed.

Miss May had been making Teeny and I guess where we were going for the duration of the drive. I laughed out loud the second we made a turn and I figured it out. Miss May turned to me with a smirk. "You know where we're going finally?"

I returned Miss May's small smile. "Yup."

"Someone tell me," Teeny said. "I hate not knowing things. That's why I try not to learn too much. As soon as you start to learn something you figure out all the stuff you need to learn, and then it's three months later and you realize you're not gonna be able to make authentic pork dumplings until you understand conversational Chinese."

Miss May chuckled. "We're going to see Salazar."

Teeny's jaw dropped. "Of course. Wow. I should have known that. Chelsea. You got that before me?"

"Only because we've come up here on prior investigations."

"Still. I should've figured that out. If I want to be part of this crime solving trio, I need to carry my weight. Even though I do weigh less than you two honkers."

"Teeny," I started, "honkers is not something they say in—"

"Britain. Yes it is," Teeny said.

Miss May interrupted our debate and made eye contact with Teeny in the rearview mirror. "Remember ten, fifteen years ago? Beth—"

"Beth was business partners with Salazar!" Teeny gasped. "They did tarot readings and they talked to the dead and did all sorts of that psychic stuff together."

"You believe in all that?" Miss May asked.

"I do and I don't," said Teeny. "I try to be open to everything so I don't get caught by surprise. But if Salazar was really an omniscient being then don't you think he'd be able to solve the mysteries before the three of us?"

"Good point," said Miss May. "Although I'm hoping this time he'll have some information that can help."

Miss May parked on the street, and we started walking into the woods. Since Salazar's fairy tale house was nestled in the woods, we could only access it by foot.

The outline of the house rose in the distance, and I remembered how truly weird and charming it was. Turrets painted like magical mushrooms. A cobblestone path leading to a massive front door. It felt like a combination of a church, a doctor's office, and a hobbit's mansion.

I heard yelling from inside the house and stopped short.

Miss May bumped into me, and Teeny bumped into her. They began to argue but I turned with an intense look in my eye, holding my finger to my lips. I whispered. "Quiet. I hear something. Salazar is yelling at someone inside."

We stood still for a moment, listening. Sure enough, I was right. The sound of raised voices emanated from the house, getting louder with each passing second.

I spotted a little shed about twenty feet away, down another cobblestone path. I gestured at it with my head. "Let's go over there. It's closer to the house. We can hide and hear what they're saying."

We hurried over to the shed and took cover behind it.

"This is a bad idea," said Teeny. "Now that we're behind the shed, it's even harder to hear."

I cringed. "You're right. But at least we're not out in the open."

I craned my neck and peered around the edge of the shed to get a better look at the house. The yelling died down. Then the front door opened.

A little, bald man stepped outside. He was wearing khaki slacks and a plaid shirt, tucked into a neat line at his waist. Salazar stood in the doorway, arms crossed. "Please do not return to my home with such quotidian demands. I deal in transcendence, not petty cash. Your energy will take days to clear."

The little man threw back his head and laughed. "You can't clear energies any more than you can tell the future or see into a little crystal ball. You owe a debt to me, and to everyone who's ever hired you — every one of your clients deserves a refund!"

That time, it was Salazar's turn to laugh. And laugh he did, for several protracted, uneasy minutes. At last, he swallowed his unsettling chuckles and his face returned to its normal placidity. "I owe you no debt. If you expect to extort me to settle your own financial troubles, I am afraid you'll be disappointed. You'll get no funds from me unless you take me to court, where I doubt you'll emerge victorious."

The little bald man scoffed. "Then I guess I'll see you in court."

The little bald man turned on his heels and charged away, down the cobblestone path, and into the woods.

Miss May, Teeny, and I watched the sedan as the man disappeared down the path. When we turned back toward the house, Salazar was standing directly above us. "Hello, ladies. Can I help you?"

Miss May raised her eyebrows. "Salazar. Hi. I'm so sorry for hiding behind your shed like this. It's just..."

"It's fine, really. I understand. You heard me arguing with that little bald devil and you wanted to avoid an awkward situation so you took cover. I would've done the same."

Teeny bit her lower lip. "How did you find us out here? How did you know? Is it... Was it because of your powers?"

Salazar shook his head. "I'm flattered. But Chelsea left her *Thomas Family Fruit and Fir Farm* tote bag leaning against the side of the shed. So I made an educated guess."

Teeny looked down. "Oh. That makes sense."

Salazar turned and headed back toward his front door. He called back over his shoulder when he got close to the entrance. "Are you three coming in or not?"

10

SHEDDING LAYERS

Salazar had been so relaxed when he found us eavesdropping behind his shed. As he let us into his home, his even-keeled energy made the hair on my neck stand up. If I had found people lurking in my yard, it would have freaked me out. Even though Salazar had been angry at his visitor moments before, he didn't seem to mind our sneaky presence at all.

I rubbed my hands on my jeans. *Yes, my palms were sweaty. We all know I sweat a lot. Doctors can't help. Trust me, I've asked.*

As we entered the front room of Salazar's home, I remembered how much I admired his taste in interior design. A beautiful bouquet of yellow tulips dominated the entryway and I wondered how he managed to keep his flower supply so fresh. *Did he pick the flowers from the woods? Did he have a flower delivery service?* I thought about asking, but we had more important inquiries.

Salazar's house was modern but still comfortable. It didn't have any stereotypical psychic or palm reader decor. The absence of mystical details actually made me trust

Salazar and his abilities more. Like he didn't have anything to prove.

Salazar took a seat in an armchair and gestured for us to sit on the couch on the opposite side of the room. "Please. Sit and be well. Relax your energies and your spirits. This is a safe space and I welcome you."

Teeny narrowed her eyes. "Why would you welcome us? You just caught us eavesdropping in your yard and hiding behind your shed like sneaky little muskrats."

Salazar chuckled. "I don't blame you. You arrived at my home, no doubt for a psychic reading or another one of my highly acclaimed services. Upon approaching my door you heard angry voices. It is no secret that the three of you are often in dangerous situations. Your instincts took over and you cowered behind the shed. I hold you blameless and I like to think I would've done the same."

Salazar reached over to the end table and switched on an old Tiffany lamp — one of a few stained glass accent pieces. The lamp give off prisms of colored light, which had a soothing impact on my senses.

"Yes," said Miss May. "We were here for those reasons, and I suppose we were acting normally, considering the circumstances. Was everything all right between you and that man? You both seemed angry."

Salazar slowly nodded his head with closed eyes, then opened them. "All is well and as it should be. It's funny how the universe works like that."

I looked over at Teeny. She rolled her eyes. "That's great. All of that universe stuff. But seriously, what was up with that guy?"

Salazar's smile faded. "It was a small dispute and I don't wish to discuss it further. Did you say you're here to procure my services?"

"Yes. We would like to take advantage of your expertise," said Miss May. "Everyone knows you're the best..."

"Mystic."

"Right. You're the best mystic in town."

"I'm the only mystic in town."

"And you're the best mystic in the area. In the tri-state region. And probably on the entire eastern seaboard."

Salazar leaned back in his chair, apparently soothed by Miss May's compliments. Funny how even people who claim to have a connection to a world greater than our own are still susceptible to vanities of the ego. "All three of you would like a psychic reading this afternoon?"

My eyes widened. The last time I had visited Salazar with Miss May, she'd forced me to do a psychic reading with him. It wasn't an experience I was eager to repeat — I was having a hard enough time with the present, I didn't need to worry about the future too. And my recent attempt at a tarot card reading had not turned out so hot.

I spoke before Miss May had the chance to throw me under the proverbial bus yet again. "We're actually not here for any readings. At least not personally. But, well, there was an incident at our orchard."

"I heard. So sad."

"It was sad," I said. "We're actually here to talk to you because this particular victim had a tarot card spread in front of her when she died."

Salazar turned his head to the side. "That's curious." He stroked his chin. "I'm not a suspect in this investigation, am I? Tarot cards are widely available for sale. You can buy them on the Internet, you can buy them in the city, I even think they sell them over at Big Jim's magic supply store in town."

"You're not a suspect," said Miss May. "We were just

hoping you could help us interpret the tarot cards that were left at the scene of the crime. We're thinking that the cards might have been a message from the killer or there might be a hidden clue in their meaning."

"I would love to help," said Salazar. "But tarot cards have many variations. I doubt you'll be able to describe the cards you saw in enough detail for me to—"

"Come on, Sal," said Teeny. "The three of us are murder mystery solving machines. We aren't about to rely only on our memories like we're just out of the bloody academy. Who do you think we are? Mr. Flowers' friends from the gardening club? Those guys could barely solve a murder if it happened right in front of them."

Salazar smiled. "You watch *Jenna and Mr. Flowers*?"

"Of course," said Teeny. "That's one of my shows. So interesting. But we're far better than some fake British TV detectives. We took a photo of the tarot card spread so you can analyze it with precision."

Miss May scooted to the edge of her chair and pulled her phone out of her purse. "I've got the picture right here. If you could take a look I think it might be helpful."

Miss May slid the phone toward Salazar but he held out his hand to stop her. "I'm sorry. I want to help. But I'm a free-lancer, as you know. And it's my moral obligation to myself and my business to make sure my services are valued."

Miss May looked over at me. I shrugged. She looked back to Salazar. "OK. How much for a tarot card reading?"

Salazar handed Miss May a little brochure the detailed his prices and services.

Miss May scanned the brochure with her pointer finger. "Seventy five dollars for a tarot card reading?"

Salazar gave Miss May a tightlipped grin. She sighed. "Fine. We'll pay it."

Over the next few minutes, Salazar struggled to process Miss May's credit card with his newfangled card reader. Then, at last, he took the phone from Miss May and looked at the tarot card spread from the murder scene.

Salazar double-tapped on the screen to zoom in on the cards. His eyes widened as he scrolled from one card to the next and he began to mutter. "Oh no. No. This..." Salazar started to hyperventilate. He stood up and dropped the phone to the floor with a loud shriek.

"Salazar! Are you OK?" Miss May asked.

Salazar pointed toward his front door. "Out. Get out."

Miss May, Teeny, and I stood.

"What happened? What did you see?" Miss May stepped toward Salazar. Once again, he pointed toward the front door. "You have brought a horrible, dangerous energy into my home. Leave now or I will call the police."

I held up my hands to calm Salazar. "Alright. We're going." I looked over at Teeny and Miss May. "Right, ladies?"

Teeny groaned. "I guess. But we did kind of pay for a tarot card reading. Now we're being kicked out without any information."

Salazar stomped on the floor. The crystal vase on the end table rattled. "Leave now."

We exited and hurried back down the path through the woods. I looked back down at Salazar's house before it vanished from view. I caught an angry glare in Salazar's eyes before he closed his curtains in a flurry. I couldn't help but wonder...

What had Salazar seen in those tarot cards? And what did it mean for our investigation?

11

TAROT TROUBLES

Miss May and I slid into our favorite booth at Teeny's restaurant, *Grandma's*, ready to discuss the investigation. *And OK, maybe ready to eat some delicious food too.*

"I always forget how stressful it is now with Salazar," I said. "That was so unsettling. One second he's calm and still, then he snaps. It's very strange to witness. Plus, we have no new information. What are we supposed to do next?"

Miss May opened her mouth to reply but Teeny cut her off. "No. We're not talking about the investigation right now."

"We need to make a plan," said Miss May. "The killer could be anywhere."

"I don't care." Teeny crossed her arms. "I have a new recipe I want you both to try it. Once we get some food in us we'll be more clearheaded. Then we can talk."

"I'm not going to argue with that," I said. "What's on the menu?"

Teeny turned back toward the kitchen and whistled. Well, she tried to whistle. All that came out was a sloppy, wet hissing sound. I laughed. Teeny glared at me. "Don't laugh. I can whistle."

Teeny put her pointer, middle finger and thumb in her mouth and blew. More spit. No sound of whistling. I laughed again.

Teeny held in a smile. "Quit laughing. Do you want your hushpuppies or not?"

I perked up in my seat. "The secret food is hushpuppies?"

Teeny hit her thigh with her palm. "Now it's not a surprise." She cupped her hands around her mouth and called out for the kitchen. "Order of puppies please!"

A pimply-faced teenage waiter approached with a covered silver platter. The teenager wore thick glasses and his voice cracked when he talked. "Puppies, as requested. The recipe is top-secret. Copyright and patent pending, in the United States and worldwide. Prepare your taste buds for a violent but gleeful assault. These hushpuppies cannot be trifled with. They come with a side of honey butter that will make your mouth water like the Hudson River. Once you eat one of Teeny's world-famous puppies you will never stop talking about them."

I giggled. The waiter had style. No doubt he had been trained by Teeny and was following a script but I liked him.

He placed the tray on the table with a flourish and remove the silver lid. There before me were two dozen of the best looking hushpuppies I had ever seen. Deep-fried, delicious cornmeal morsels rested beside a little bowl of whipped honey butter. The smell was sweet and savory at the same time and I could just tell they were crispy on the outside and moist on the inside.

"Don't just look at them," said Teeny. "Try one."

I grabbed a puppy, dipped it in the honey butter, and put

the whole thing in my mouth. I suddenly felt as though I were receiving a full body massage. My bones relaxed. My stomach warmed. My eyes closed. "Oh my." I spoke slowly, like I was in the middle of falling asleep. "That's the best thing I've ever tasted."

Teeny smiled her giant smile and clapped her tiny, rapid golf claps. "I knew you would like them. I spent weeks on the recipe. They've got buttermilk and cornmeal. Some flour, and a little bit of sugar. Baking soda. Obviously, salt. Oh! And onions and green onions too. What do you think, May?"

Teeny and I looked over at Miss May. Like me, she looked like she was falling asleep, having a beautiful half-dream. She chewed in silence. Teeny nudged her. "May. Tell me you love my pups."

Miss May opened her eyes. "I love your hushpuppies."

"Great. Scoot over. I want some." Teeny slid into the booth beside Miss May and popped a hush puppy in her mouth. She turned to the waiter who still stood awkwardly beside the table. "You can go now, Samuel. Good job."

Samuel give us a small, polite bow and exited with a strange, peppy little walk. "Weird kid," said Teeny. "But I'm impressed. He remembered all his lines."

"I'm going to eat one more hush puppy or five then we should talk about what happened at Salazar's," said Miss May.

I plunked a few hushpuppies on my plate and nodded. "I can eat and talk at the same time. But I don't have that much more to say. The whole experience freaked me out."

Teeny nodded. "That guy is sketched out. That's the expression, right Chelsea?"

"He's sketchy."

"It all seemed fake to me," said Teeny. "I don't know if I

even believe he has any special abilities. I think he plays up the theatrics to get people talking because he knows that any publicity is good publicity, especially in a small town like Pine Grove."

Miss May dipped a hush puppy in honey butter. "Cynical."

Teeny shrugged. "Practical. Think about it... He didn't provide any information about the tarot cards in the photo. He just got all panicked and made us leave."

"I suppose you're right," I said. "Salazar didn't help us decipher the tarot cards at all. But that doesn't mean we should stop pursuing the meaning of the cards."

"I agree," said Miss May. "I have an important question... Do you think Beth was providing a reading to the person who killed her? Or do we think Beth was receiving a reading from another tarot card reader before she was killed?"

I shook my head. "I have no idea. The cards were in the middle of the table. I hadn't even thought of that. It could go either way. I researched tarot cards on my phone earlier but there's so much to learn. I didn't read anything that helps much."

Miss May nodded. "We need to find another expert to help us translate those cards. But I have a hunch we can wait to pursue that further."

"OK," I said. "What do you think we should do instead?"

"Beth lived two towns over. So we hardly know anything about her, right?"

Teeny nodded. "The three of us know what everyone in town knows. She was a little wacky. She had a funky smell. And she came to Pine Grove pretty regularly to drink coffee and walk around babbling."

"Like I said," Miss May reiterated. "We don't know much

about her. So I think we should go by her place tomorrow and see what we can find out."

I dipped my pointer finger in the honey butter than licked the butter off. "You think we're going to have to break in?"

Miss May moved her eyes. "It's not like we've never done it before."

12

TWO TOWNS OVER

Miss May guided her big yellow Volkswagen bus over toward Beth's house with confidence. Although Beth lived in Blue Mountain, about a fifteen minute drive from the center of Pine Grove, Miss May seemed to know the route by heart.

"How do you know where Beth lives again?" I asked.

"A few years ago she broke her leg in a bicycle accident. Remember that, Teeny?"

Teeny nodded. "I had totally forgotten until you just mentioned it. Oh boy. She was riding through Pine Grove. Had her head in the clouds and drove her bicycle right into the sewer."

My eyes widened and I tried not to laugh. "How did she manage that?"

"Mayor Delgado was on her big sewer improvement kick. She had all the manholes opened in town for days. Most of us residents, we knew to avoid them," Miss May said. "Blue Mountain people... Not so much."

Teeny tittered. "It's not funny. I know it's not funny. But I still remember the sound of Beth yelling from inside that sewer."

Miss May chuckled. "Oh, me too. 'Help! I've fallen into the sewer. Someone help me out of the sewer.'"

Teeny shook her head. "It took half the fire department to figure out how to pull her out of that hole. I think they ended up using a horse harness or something like that."

"They did not use a horse harness, Teeny." Miss May looked in the rearview mirror and smiled. "They dropped a ladder down."

Teeny held up a pointer finger. "That's right. They dropped the ladder down but Beth was too afraid to climb up so they had to send a couple firemen down there to talk her into it."

"That's a bizarre story. But I still don't understand how that bicycle injury helped you figure out where she lives in Blue Mountain," I said.

"Right. I knew we were talking about something," said Miss May. "I felt bad for the poor girl after she fell in that sewer, so I volunteered to bring food over to her a few times a week. Blue Mountain is such a small town. They don't have the same community resources as Pine Grove. I wanted her to know that our town was sorry for trapping her in the sewer."

"But I thought you barely knew Beth."

"That's true," said Miss May. "I brought food over there maybe a dozen times. But she never opened the door and there was never a light on in the house. There was always a note on the front door that said 'please leave food here,' and that's it."

Teeny shuddered. "That girl always gave me the creepy-deepies."

"I think you mean heebie-jeebies," I said.

"I said it how I meant it," said Teeny. "The British way."

Miss May pointed out the windshield. "That's it. That's her house right there."

Beth's home was an old colonial. It had two stories and it was covered in peeling, white paint. The front yard was dotted with buckets and rusty, forgotten tools. A broken window had been repaired with a square of plywood.

"Not really charming, is it?" said Teeny.

Miss May parked and we hopped out of the car. "It never was."

Miss May trudged through tall grasses around the back of the house. Teeny and I followed. I called ahead to Miss May as we walked. "You don't even want to try the front door?"

Miss May called back to me over her shoulder. "I don't think it would help if we rang the bell, Chelsea. Pretty sure Beth isn't home."

I looked down. *Oh yeah. We were visiting the home of a murder victim.*

"Besides, she never used the front door. She had me bring food around back, and I think she entered and exited that way as well."

We turned the corner to the back of the house to find a large sunroom. The screen door that led into the sunroom was ajar. Miss May held it open and stepped aside for me and Teeny to enter. "After you."

The sunroom, like the front yard, was cluttered with rusty old tools and dozens of random planters and flowerpots. Miss May looked around inside. "I don't think a single item has moved since I last came here three years ago."

"Can I help you?" A gruff voice rang out from nearby.

The door that went from the sunroom into the house opened and a tall, skinny man stepped out. He had a neat beard and an (understandably) angry look in his eye.

Miss May stammered. "Hi. I'm so sorry. I know this must seem like an awkward intrusion. But I was a friend of Beth's."

Teeny stepped forward. "Me too. We used to bring her food after she fell into that sewer in Pine Grove?"

"That's right," said Miss May. "And I was so distraught to hear what happened to her. I wanted to come by and visit this place one last time to pay my respects."

The tall man crossed his arms. "This isn't a memorial. It's my home."

"Right. My apologies," Miss May said. "I'm so sorry. And you are..."

"I'm Beth's brother, Michael."

Miss May nodded. "Of course. Michael. Beth told me all about you. After the sewer accident we got close. She told me she had a wonderful brother."

"Who are you people?" A chubby bald man approached from the backyard carrying two black suits, fresh from the dry cleaners.

I swallowed a gasp of surprise. The chubby bald man was the same person we had seen arguing with Salazar. I looked over at Miss May. I could tell she also noticed, but she kept her cool.

Michael opened the door for the little bald man and took the dry cleaning. "These women were friends of Beth's."

The little bald man frowned. "Beth didn't have any friends other than us. And she only liked us some of the time. I can't believe she's never coming back to this house."

Michael looked down. "Me too." He held out the dry

cleaning at arm's length to get a better look at it. "But at least we'll look good for the funeral. Thanks for picking this up."

"Those are beautiful suits," said Teeny. "I can tell from here. Well-made. And they look like they're going to fit you both perfectly."

"We should go," said Miss May. "I'm late for my reading with Salazar. Please accept our condolences."

Miss May took a step toward the back door. The chubby man blocked her path. "Hold on a second. You seriously believe that hack Salazar has some sort of special powers? He's a liar and a cheat."

Michael put a hand on his brother's arm. "Jonathan. It's OK. Let them go."

Jonathan shook Michael off. "No. I can't send people off to that clown in good conscience. Do you know what he did to my sister?"

Miss May stammered. "Not... Not exactly, no."

"She worked for him at that little mushroom palace for years. She did readings, palm work, everything. But he owed her hundreds of dollars and he never paid up. Thousands, even. Who knows how much? It's ridiculous. Now she's dead and I know he'll never pay the money."

The chubby man's face reddened. Michael stayed calm. "It's OK, Jonathan."

"It is not OK. We need that cash to pay for this funeral. Someone dies you at least want to give them a good funeral." Jonathan dabbed a tear from his eye. "I'm sorry. I have to go inside."

Jonathan stormed into the house and closed the door with a slam. Michael took a few moments to steady himself then turned back to us. "It's a hard time. Forgive me. Will we be seeing you at the funeral?"

Teeny gave Michael an awkward smile. "Wouldn't miss it

for the world."

13

EULOGY EUREKA

Beth's funeral took place on Monday afternoon at the *Gates of Heaven Cemetary* in Pine Grove. Up to that point in our amateur sleuth careers, Miss May and I had mostly avoided attending the funerals of the victims of murders we investigated. We'd had some bad experiences with loved ones of the deceased in the past, and it felt rather crass to crash someone's memorial in service of sleuthing.

But in the case of the murdered tarot card reader, we hadn't been left much of a choice. Beth's brothers, Michael and Jonathan, clearly needed support during that hard time. And Miss May insisted we attend even though I kind of begged her to let me stay home.

"We already said we would go," Miss May had said. "Besides, we might pick up an important clue during the services."

I felt distracted for much of the service. Nobody likes attending funerals (at least nobody I know) but for me, every funeral conjured up the sharp sorrow of losing my parents. Although I'd recently gotten some closure on their deaths, I still didn't like the sense memories associated with attending funerals.

I snapped out of my self-pity party as a small, fastidious woman began to deliver Beth's eulogy. The woman wore small, black-framed glasses and her salt-and-pepper hair had been cut close to her head, almost in a buzz cut. She spoke in short, clipped sentences and barely moved her mouth when she talked.

"Friends, family, neighbors, " she began, "this is a sad day. Beth was a true bright spot in my life and the lives of many others. She and I met when we were undergraduates at Harvard University and we have been best friends ever since that day."

When the small woman mentioned Harvard University, I looked over at Miss May. She shrugged. Neither of us had had any idea Beth was a Harvard graduate, and I think we were both surprised.

But Beth's Harvard status was not the only surprising fact featured in the eulogy. The small woman went on to reveal that Beth had been to jail for political protest. She also claimed that Beth had lived in France for three years. And the woman also seemed to imply that Beth spoke multiple languages including Japanese and Farsi. The eulogy concluded with the woman offering a plea to Beth's spirit, requesting that Beth always remember, "laughter at the edge of the rainbow, the painted lady with her gorgeous nails, and the traitor at the end of the bar."

After the funeral, Miss May, Teeny, and I headed back to the big yellow VW bus. But Miss May stopped in her tracks when she noticed a commotion at the other end of the parking lot. The woman who had delivered the eulogy was in an argument with a large, sloppy man. The man looked out of place in blue jeans and a tattered T-shirt. He yelled and pointed at the small woman and she yelled and pointed back.

Miss May squinted in their direction. "Is that Big Jim from the magic shop?"

Teeny put her hand to her forehead like a sailor scanning the horizon. "Looks like it. That weird little lady doesn't look too happy with him."

I cringed. "We don't have to go over there, do we?"

Miss May glanced at me like a disapproving teacher. And I knew we had to go.

Big Jim spotted us as we approached and immediately turned to us for some sort of validation. "Miss May. You're a de facto leader in this community. Talk some sense into this little lady. Tell her to calm down."

"What's going on?" Miss May inquired.

"This man made Beth's life miserable. He made her career and her psychic abilities into a joke when he decided to open that magic shop. As soon as that place was open for business, Large James here started telling everyone that Beth was a charlatan and a liar. He sold tarot cards like playing cards. He made her into a fool by hawking his wares with such casual nonchalance."

Big Jim shrugged. "I'm a magician. I sell magic kits. I teach lessons. Yes, I think the psychic industry is nonsense. It's a business just like mine. I won't apologize for making that known."

The little woman stepped toward Big Jim. "You take that back. Beth was not some capitalist pig like you. She was sharing her gift. And because of you, no one in this region took her seriously. Now she's been murdered. She's dead and she'll never gain the respect she deserved."

Beth's tall, skinny brother, Michael, approached in his crisp black suit. "Lillian. It's OK. Big Jim knows he was wrong. I can see it in his eyes as clearly as you can. I think that needs to be enough for today. For Beth."

Lillian looked over at Michael. She sighed. "It's not fair, Mike."

Michael put his arm around Lillian and led her away. "It's not fair, you're right. But he doesn't deserve any more of your time."

Miss May, Teeny, Big Jim, and I watched as Michael led Lillian over to her car. Big Jim grumbled. "She's a psychopath just like her friend Beth was."

Miss May shot a look at Big Jim. "May she rest in peace."

14

IN THE WAKE OF THE WAKE

After the funeral, Miss May and I had to head back to the farm to help KP with the peach harvest. Teeny went back to her restaurant for the afternoon rush. And we all promised we wouldn't talk too much about what happened at the funeral until we met up again later.

Back on the orchard, Miss May and KP had a meeting in her office. I sat there quietly for the first fifteen minutes as they talked facts and figures and discussed the harvest. Then I excused myself because honestly, I was bored. I had done well in my business classes at school but that didn't mean I liked them. I wanted to check on my animals, so that's what I did.

First, I visited our tiny horse, See-Saw, down in the barn. See-Saw was miniature in size but gargantuan in wisdom, and I often liked to discuss cases with her. Huffing, neighing, snorting, and swishing her tail, she offered valuable feedback no matter the situation.

That day, I fed See-Saw some grass and filled her in on the details of Beth's murder. But before See-Saw had anything good to say about the case, she started to whinny and point her head at the barn door.

I turned to look and there was Detective Wayne Hudson leaning against the door jamb. "Hey, Chelsea. I didn't want to interrupt."

"Wayne. You should have interrupted. Now you seem like you are just weirdly standing there and eavesdropping. Were you trying to pick up information about the murderer?"

Wayne shook his head. "Certainly not. And why would you have information, anyway? You wouldn't be investigating this case, now would you?"

I rolled my eyes. It was preposterous that Wayne continued to act like Miss May and I were not expert sleuths. But, I reasoned, it was part of his job description to deter us from "interfering," and I suspected that he was playing dumb at least partially to give us the space we needed to conduct our investigation. If Wayne "didn't know" we were sleuthing, he didn't have to report us or try to stop us.

"Good point," I said. "We're not investigating anything. But what are you doing here if it's not about our investigation that's not happening?" *Some people put their foot in their mouth... I put my entire leg in there.*

"I went by *Grandma's* and Teeny said you were up here. Wanted to make sure you're safe, since your keys are still missing. I thought you and your aunt decided to stay with Teeny."

"We've been sleeping over at Teeny's but we still need to run the orchard. KP likes to think he can do it alone, but everybody needs help sometimes. Plus, See-Saw likes extra treats."

See-Saw swished her tail in agreement.

"So nothing suspicious has been going on up here?"

See-Saw munched another handful of grass. I looked at her to avoid staring directly into Wayne's eyes. "No. How's everything going with you?"

"Not bad. I got a new TV. Fifty-five inches. Not that I'm some guy who's obsessed with the size of his TV. But it's good for sports.... Let's see, what else? I've been cooking. Trying to eat healthy. Lots of broccoli."

I laughed. "I meant... How are things going with the investigation?"

Wayne blushed. "Oh. Of course. Good. Everything is fine. It's all going according to plan. And the plan is to catch the killer so that's good."

Wayne's walkie-talkie buzzed with activity. He grabbed it, turned away from me, and muttered something. Then he turned back to me. "I need to run. Good to see you, Chelsea."

I smirked. "Keep eating those vegetables."

I hung out with See-Saw for a little while longer. I could tell she wanted to gossip about Wayne. See-Saw always insisted on knowing every detail of my life. I maintained that Wayne and I were only friends. Which was true. We were barely friends, in fact. Sometimes enemies. And I had a boyfriend, even if he was in Africa with the lions.

After I left See-Saw, I took a walk with Steve, who limped and loped along happily. Then I fed Kitty, who glared disdainfully at her food for a long moment before begrudgingly eating a few bites. She wasn't getting enough attention, and she wanted me to know that she wasn't happy about it.

Finally, as the sun began to set, I headed back up toward the farmhouse. Teeny and Miss May were already sitting on the steps, chatting.

"I thought we weren't going to discuss the case until we were all together again," I said.

"We're not discussing the case," said Miss May. "We're talking about Wayne."

Teeny cackled. "I heard he paid you a little visit today. How did he look? Good? Strong?"

I looked down. "He looked fine. He's been eating a lot of broccoli."

Teeny and Miss May exchanged an excited glance. Miss May turned back to me. "What is that supposed to mean?"

I backpedaled for a few minutes and tried to avoid all their prying questions. Then I turned the conversation to the investigation and Beth's funeral. "Everything that happened at the funeral seemed strange to me," I said. "And the more we learn about Beth, the more confused I am."

"Same," said Teeny. "I thought Beth was a bat hanging on the roof of the cave talking nonsense to the other bats."

"Is that how they say 'batty' in Britain?" I asked.

Teeny smirked and ignored my snark. "But now I learn she's worldly and Harvard educated? Honestly, kinda made me feel bad about myself. I don't speak any other languages unless I'm ordering takeout and even then I pronounce everything wrong."

"I agree," said Miss May. "That eulogy threw me off. I've never seen that Lillian woman before. And Beth's brothers said Beth didn't have any friends."

"And what was up with that fight between Lillian and Big Jim?" I asked. "Beth was fighting with Big Jim too."

Miss May fluttered her eyelashes in disbelief. "I guess Big Jim approaches his magic and psychic readings and all that like it's a business. He doesn't act like people in those professions are special or gifted in any way. And that offends Lillian because it discredited Beth."

I scratched my face. “Still. It was strange for her to attack Jim like that at the funeral.”

Teeny rubbed her chin. “It was strange for Big Jim to attend the funeral dressed in his yardwork clothes.”

I sat on the step right between Teeny and Miss May. “And what about how Lillian mentioned in her eulogy that Beth had been to prison?”

Miss May scooted over to give me a little more room. “That’s right! Lillian said Beth had gone to jail for some kind of protest, but I never knew Beth to be too political. I guess I didn’t really know Beth at all.”

Teeny straightened her posture. “What if that was a lie? What if Beth went to jail for something nefarious. Maybe Beth was murdered by someone who’s connected to her criminal past.”

Miss May ran her tongue over her teeth. “That’s a little far-fetched but it’s not impossible.”

“It happens on *Jenna and Mr. Flowers* all the time,” said Teeny. “Not that exactly but stuff like that. And you know my TV shows have been helpful in our investigations in the past. Don’t tell me I’m wrong about that.”

Miss May held up her hands. “I’m not going to talk about your TV shows right now.”

“The ones on the British channels are serious. They’re basically journalism.”

“Let’s stay focused on the suspects,” I said. “I agree it could be someone from Beth’s past, criminal or not. Sounds like Salazar owed money to her or her brothers that he didn’t want to pay, so he’s a suspect as well. And I think we should also consider Big Jim a suspect. He obviously disliked and disrespected Beth, so maybe there’s more to their relationship than meets the third eye. And she accused him of wanting to kill her.”

"You're right," said Miss May. "What about the brothers? Do we think they could've done it?"

Teeny slapped her head with her palm. "I almost forgot. I got to the funeral a little early today and I heard the funeral director arguing with those creepy brothers about money. Apparently their check bounced and they needed to figure it out or the funeral director was going to refuse to bury Beth."

"That's absurd," said Miss May. "You can't hold someone's burial plot hostage in their time of need."

"I agree," said Teeny. "But...suppose there was some financial incentive for the brothers if Beth died... That could be motivation."

I looked from Teeny to Miss May. "So there are a few suspects. Who should we focus on first?"

"Not sure," said Miss May.

A delivery truck pulled up in the driveway and Miss May stood to greet it.

An African American man jumped out and approached us, carrying a small brown package. I didn't recognize the man so I assumed he was filling in for our normal driver, Sandra. He had a nice face and I liked him right away.

Miss May signed for the package and made small talk. "Beautiful night, isn't it?"

The delivery man nodded. "It'll be even more beautiful when I get back home to my armchair."

Miss May chuckled. "Sounds like a plan to me. You're out a little late tonight, aren't you?"

The man shook his head. "Don't get me started. Two flat tires in a single day. I should have been finished with my runs two hours ago. You're my last delivery."

"Get on home," said Miss May. "Is Sandra out sick?"

"She'll be back tomorrow."

Miss May crossed back to the front steps as she opened the package with a pocketknife. I was curious about what was in the box and I looked excitedly over Miss May's shoulder.

"What is it?"

Miss May pulled out a classic, black and white marble notebook from the package.

"It's a notebook," said Miss May. "And it's got Beth's name on the cover..."

15

CURSE SMURSE

We went inside the farmhouse, sat at the kitchen table, and gathered around Beth's notebook. Miss May held the notebook and Teeny and I sat on either side of her, probably too close. But that notebook was the most mysterious and intriguing clue we had ever received. It was at least in the top five. I wanted to see every word.

The first page contained a note from Beth. The handwriting was severe and angular. Beth had pressed so hard with her red pen that in some places she had scratched right through the page and on to the one behind it.

"To whom it may concern,

The contents of this notebook do not concern you. This notebook is the property of Beth and it has all of her ideas and secrets. Any who reads the contents herein shall be cursed in perpetuity throughout the universe."

I gulped. "Any who reads this book shall be cursed? Are we sure we want to be reading this?"

"The woman was already murdered, Chelsea," Teeny

said. "How much creepier could this get? I say we keep going."

Miss May nodded. "I agree."

"It could get a lot creepier, you guys," I said. "If Beth really had paranormal powers, she could be cursing us right now…from beyond the grave!"

"Oh, that's a bunch of biscuits," Teeny said. "Curse-smurse." Then she added, "Biscuit is how they say cookie in Britain."

"Forget about the curse. Notice anything else odd about this note so far?" Miss May asked.

I shrugged. "Beth pressed down really hard when she wrote but that doesn't surprise me. Uh, also that phrase, 'in perpetuity throughout the universe' is striking. Seems official, like something I read in the one pre-law class I took in college."

Miss May nodded. "It's legalese, for sure."

"Maybe she really did go to Harvard," said Teeny. "Let's keep reading."

The rest of the note had been written entirely in capital letters. "BETH SEES ALL AND KNOWS ALL. THIS IS AN ACCURATE RECORD OF HER DAILY LIFE. ONE DAY THIS NOTEBOOK WILL BE A TREASURED ARTIFACT HOUSED IN A WORLD CLASS MUSEUM."

"Little full of herself, wasn't she?" Teeny shook her head. "How do you know your life story is going to be an artifact in a museum?"

"She was insane, Teeny," I pointed out.

Teeny shook her head. "That's no excuse to be so cocky. It's just unseemly, that's what it is."

Miss May turned the page. The heading on the top of the page read: DAY ONE. It was the same scratchy handwriting. But the day Beth described on the page seemed mundane and far from spectacular.

I read her writing out loud. "Woke up. Ate two bananas. Rode my bike. Went to get coffee at the *Brown Cow* and had a great conversation with Brian. He is a Sagittarius. The end."

Miss May flipped through several pages. "They're all like that. Simple descriptions of whatever boring stuff she did that day."

"Hold on. Go back a few pages. I thought I saw a list or something." I pointed at the notebook and Miss May flipped back five or six pages. I caught her arm. "There. Stop."

Sure enough, there in the middle of the notebook was a page titled "PEOPLE WHO I KNOW FOR A FACT WANT TO KILL ME."

Miss May shook her head. "This poor woman thought everyone was out to get her."

I leaned forward. "So you don't think this could be a viable list of suspects?"

Miss May shrugged. "Let's see. The first person listed here is Tom Gigley. Gigley has never wanted to kill anyone."

"That's not true," said Teeny. "That one time he wanted to kill everyone who worked at the cable company."

"He didn't actually want to kill the cable employees," I contended. "He just sent them death threats, that's all."

"Apparently Beth thinks Gigley wanted to kill her because," Miss May read, "and I quote 'he parked his car next to mine today and it was very aggressive and I know it was a sign that he wants me dead.'"

"Fine," said Teeny. "Maybe Tom isn't a real suspect."

I bit my lower lip. "Who else is on the list?"

"The next person is Humphrey," Miss May said. "That man is three hundred and fifty years old. He's not a killer."

"Don't let your personal affection for these people cloud your investigative mind," I said. "We've suspected Humphrey before...in the Santa slaying."

"Who else do you think wanted her dead?" asked Teeny.

Miss May scanned down the list with her finger. "Looks like...everyone in town. And these reasons Beth has listed are absurd. She suspects Petey wanted to kill her because she found a bone in her fish at *Peter's Land and Sea*. She thinks the mayor wanted to kill her because she violated a thirty minute parking rule. Hold on a second...She thinks Sudeer Patel wanted to kill her too. And next to him she's only written the word 'revenge.'"

"And she pressed so hard when she was writing his name that she ripped the page," Teeny pointed out. "Do you think that she wronged Sudeer? Did she steal from him or try to seduce his wife? Maybe she kidnapped him or broke into his house and stole the lunch right out from under his hands."

Miss May closed the notebook. "Who knows what Beth might have done to Sudeer. But this is a clue worth following up on."

"So we need to talk to Sudeer," I said.

"And find out why he wanted revenge on a dead woman," Teeny said.

16

HERE, HERE, SUDEER

I stood up from the table and pulled on my light jacket. "Let's get to the bottom of this. Let's get past the bottom. To the middle."

Teeny scrunched up her nose. "The middle comes before the bottom."

"Not in my imagination," I said. "First there's the top, then there's the bottom and last of all comes the middle. You know what? When I say it out loud it doesn't make any sense. But think about the middle of the earth. It's way past the bottom!"

"It doesn't matter anyway," said Miss May. "It's after dark on Monday night. If Sudeer did this, which I don't think he did, then our arrival at his house will freak him out. And if he's innocent, it's just rude to visit a family man out of nowhere on Monday night. We should go tomorrow."

"Works for me," said Teeny. "You girls ready to head back to my place? I'm all set up for an old-fashioned slumber party."

I laughed. I hadn't been over to Teeny's house for a slumber party since I was a little girl. Yes, I'd been sleeping there for the last few nights, but a real slumber party was a whole different story. "I can't wait."

Teeny had not been kidding when she said it was time for a slumber party. Her entire kitchen table was covered with different shades of nail polish. She had three bottles of cheap white wine chilling in the refrigerator. And she had made a huge tray of brownies for us to "nosh up while we gossip."

"This is going to be so much fun." Teeny picked up a light pink shade of nail polish. "I think I want this color on my fingers. But then something fun on my toes."

I chuckled. "Light pink isn't fun enough for your toes?"

"You know what I mean," said Teeny. "I want something sparkly."

Miss May kicked off her shoes. "These toes have never seen nail polish and they never will. But I'd love a brownie."

Miss May plucked a plump brownie off the tray and collapsed onto Teeny's overstuffed sofa. As soon as my aunt bit into her brownie, she gasped. "Teeny. You're a better baker than I am! How is this so gooey on the inside?"

"You like it?"

I grabbed the brownie and took a bite. The thing was incredible. Transcendent. "You're on a roll lately. This might be even better than the hushpuppies."

Teeny narrowed her eyes. "What's wrong with the hushpuppies?"

My mouth was full but I talked anyway. "No. Nothing. Those are incredible too. Just different tastes."

Over the next hour or two, Teeny told us old stories as she and I painted each others' nails and ate brownies. I loved hearing Teeny's stories about her youth.

Unlike a lot of small town folk, she had done a surprising amount of traveling. Teeny had even hitchhiked in her 20's and ended up in San Francisco. She'd stayed there for a few months but then missed Pine Grove, so she came back, as she said, "With more than a few flowers in my hair. Don't worry. I showered."

The next morning, we piled into Teeny's pink convertible and headed over to Sudeer's office in the business district of Pine Grove. *OK. "Business district" might be a strong word.* But there were businesses there. Sudeer had a little architectural firm office across the street from the coffee shop, *The Brown Cow*. That was essentially the entire district. When we pulled up, there weren't any other cars in the parking lot.

Miss May climbed out of the convertible and squinted toward the office. "That's odd. It's 10 AM. Sudeer should already be here for the day."

"Maybe he stayed up late painting his toenails and had trouble waking up this morning," said Teeny with a yawn.

Miss May approached the office. "Come on. Maybe he walked to work today." She pulled on the door handle but the door did not open. "This is so weird. Sudeer must not be in there."

I cupped my hands to peer into the front window. "I don't think Sudeer has been in his office for a while."

Teeny and Miss May stood on either side of me, cupping their hands around their eyes to get a better look inside, just like I had. "What makes you say that?" Miss May asked.

"Look at the wall. All the electronics have been unplugged from the outlets."

"Maybe he wanted to preserve power," said Teeny. "That's just smart and frugal."

"Perhaps," I said. "But usually people only unplug their electronics when they plan to be away for a long time."

Miss May squatted gracelessly and kept peering inside.

"Look at these windowsills. There's visible dust. Sudeer takes such pride in his office. It surprises me that he'd let it gather dust."

Teeny turned away from the window and paced. "You're right. Sudeer was so proud when he opened this place. You know he kept it clean because he used the same cleaning crew that my sister Peach uses at the inn. They're the best in town."

"Computers unplugged. Dust on the windowsill," I said. "Sudeer stopped coming to this office."

"I think you're right, Chelsea." Miss May pulled a brownie out of her purse and nibbled on the corner. "But the question is why?"

17

AN ARCHITECT OF REVENGE

Sudeer lived in the *Hastings Pond* neighborhood of Pine Grove. Although he had always been an important part of Pine Grove's business community, and I had enjoyed getting to know Sudeer over the past year, he often came up as a suspect in our investigations.

Up to that point, he hadn't been guilty of any murders in town. He was a kind, upstanding family man. At least to the untrained eye. But I knew better than to trust an untrained eye. My year as a sleuth had taught me that even the most unthinkable suspects could be killers. So as we approached in Teeny's little convertible that morning, I had a strong case of the deja-vu sweats.

"Should we make a plan before we question Sudeer?" I picked at the pink nail polish on my thumb.

"We can tell him he won a sweepstakes and we're the congratulations committee," said Teeny. "Everyone loves to win stuff."

Miss May shook her head. "Sudeer knows us too well for that. As soon as he sees us, he's going to know why we're here. It's our job to question him and hunt for clues. If we're observant, I think we'll be able to pick up on the truth, whether that's good, bad, or in the middle."

"Now is the middle after bad or between good and bad?" I asked.

"The middle is whatever you want it to be." Miss May pointed out the window. "We're here."

Sudeer's cottage was one story. It had a little white picket fence and a perfect little green lawn. Miss May rang the doorbell and we waited. I heard happy squeals of laughter from inside and remembered Sudeer's adorable little children. A female voice called out from inside and I heard footsteps approach. "One second."

Kayla, Sudeer's wife, took a few seconds to quiet the children then opened the door with a smile. Her smile faded when she saw we were her visitors. "Miss May, Chelsea, Teeny. Don't tell me my husband is a suspect again."

Miss May reached into her purse and pulled out an apple pie. "I brought you a pie."

Kayla pushed the pie away. "I don't want your pie. Sudeer is not a killer. Not now, not before, not ever in the future. I don't want you around here. We're having a nice family breakfast."

"I'm sorry, Kayla," said Miss May. "It's unfortunate that our investigations keep leading us back to your door. I know that must be frustrating."

"Frustrating is an understatement. I hate seeing your faces."

"No need to be rude, Kayla," said Teeny. "May offered you a pie. She clearly feels bad."

Kayla began to close the door. "I don't care if she feels bad. My husband is not a killer."

Miss May stopped the door with her foot. "You're right. I don't think Sudeer is a killer. But I think he might have information that could help us find the killer. Which will make Pine Grove safer for all of us."

"No. Sorry. If the police come here and have a warrant then they can talk to my husband. But I don't want him anywhere near the three of you."

Miss May sighed. "If we spoke for a few minutes I'm sure we'd find that Sudeer is innocent and has some reasonable and elucidating explanation for his connection to the victim. Please. Five minutes."

A male hand grabbed the door and opened it all the way. There stood Sudeer, wearing a full set of matching flannel pajamas. He held an adorable toddler in his arms. Neither of them looked like a cold-blooded murderer. "It's OK, Kayla. I'll talk."

Kayla fumed and stormed back into the house. Sudeer stood aside with a soft, exhausted smile. "Please. Come in."

Miss May, Teeny, Sudeer, and I sat across from one another on floral couches in his cramped living room. I admired the photos of his babies on the wall. But when my gaze returned back to Sudeer's face, I felt uneasy. I knew he didn't really want us there, and whether or not he was a killer, his displeasure at our presence weighed on me.

Miss May started by apologizing and giving a quick summary of why we were there. Sudeer seemed understanding but impatient. His toddlers were all calling out for their "da-da" from the other room and Kayla often walked into the living room, glared at us, then exited back to the kitchen.

Finally, after some chitchat, Miss May boiled everything down to one question. "You weren't at the peach party at the orchard. But that doesn't exonerate you. Beth's notebook claims you wanted to kill her. And she didn't turn up dead until hours after the party. So please... Tell me....

Where were you between the hours of 8 pm and 3 am that night?"

Sudeer stammered. "That's a large window. I... I don't know. I was at my office."

Miss May looked down. "We were just there, Sudeer. We went to look for you at your office first because we didn't want to bother you at home. But...it looks like the place has been shut down for some time."

Sudeer switched gears fast. "I was at my home office. Here. Of course, I was here at home. I probably went to bed around 10 or 11. I said I was at my office but I didn't mean my office in town. You get that, right?"

Miss May looked up at Sudeer and narrowed her eyes. "OK. Do you want to tell me why you haven't been at your actual office for a little while?"

I could tell Miss May was not buying Sudeer's story. I don't think any of us were. Working these murder investigations had taught us how to detect a person's lies. But Sudeer was so visibly anxious, our expertise was hardly necessary.

"It's not worth the money," Sudeer said. "I'm just one person with occasional help. I don't need a whole office in town."

"If that were true, why not put the place up for rent?" Miss May crossed her legs.

"That's a good question. I'm looking into it. Going to rent it. I'm going to rent it soon and that's just the whole story."

Miss May exhaled. "Sudeer. Tell us the truth."

Kayla appeared and stood in the doorway, arms crossed. Sudeer looked over at her and she nodded. "OK. I had problems with Beth. It wasn't a big deal. But she came in one day and asked if I could build her a house. At that point, I didn't know who she was. I was friendly with her and asked how I could help. She came back by my office every day for a month. Always with questions about this house she wanted to build, but never ready to make a deposit or officially hire me as her architect. Well one day, I confronted her about it. I told her my time is valuable and if she wasn't serious about hiring me, then I needed her to stop making so many appointments and showing up at my work. That was when things got strange. Beth accused me of breaking her heart. She said we had a special connection and we were in love. She was furious that I tried to 'modify' our relationship and she screamed at me. She wanted me to leave Kayla for her. Thankfully, Beth never managed to find out where I live. So I stopped going to the office and I started working from home."

Miss May nodded. "So Beth threatened you and your family."

Sudeer put up his hands. "No. No, no, I didn't look at her as a threat. If anything, I felt bad for her. I wanted her to go away but I didn't want her to die."

Kayla stepped further into the room. "My husband is not a killer."

"You mentioned," I muttered.

"OK," said Miss May. She turned back to Sudeer. "Can I ask you this one more time... Where were you Saturday night between the hours of 8 PM and 3 AM?"

"I know where he was." Kayla's eyes glimmered.

Sudeer spun to face her. "You do?"

Kayla smirked. "You can't keep any secrets from me, Sudeer."

Teeny threw up her hands. "So where was he?"

"There's a jewelry store down in Brooklyn that's open late. It's owned by a strange family with sporadic hours, and they have the most beautiful pieces. Sudeer knew I had been stressed by this Beth ordeal. So he went down there

Saturday night and bought me an incredible necklace." Kayla's eyes welled up. "Sudeer is a good husband and a good man. And he has wonderful taste in jewelry."

Kayla pulled the receipt from her pocket. She handed it to Miss May. "He bought the necklace late Saturday night. You can see the timestamp on the receipt. There's no way he could have been back in Pine Grove until 2 AM at the earliest. He didn't kill that woman."

Sudeer hung his head. "I can't believe you knew about the necklace! It was supposed to be a surprise."

Kayla crossed and gave Sudeer a big hug. "Of course I knew. You left the receipt in your pants pocket when I did the laundry." They separated and Kayla turned to us. "Now, you three need to leave or I'm calling the police."

"We'll go," said Miss May. "But if you had proof of Sudeer's innocence this whole time, why didn't you show us when we arrived?"

"I didn't want to ruin his surprise if I could help it. But you three would never leave here if I didn't have proof," Kayla made a shooing motion with her hands. "Do you need me to show you the door?"

Clearly, it was time for us to leave. We exited without further ado.

Even though we'd learned Sudeer's story, I felt worse than I had before. Beth had been an aggressive and erratic woman. She'd wreaked havoc on many people's lives. And any one of those people could have wanted her dead.

18

SECRET INGREDIENTS

We drove through town after leaving Sudeer's, and Teeny insisted we stop by her restaurant. We were all hungry, so she didn't really have to twist our arms about it. We headed over to *Grandma's* to grab some food and talk about the case. As soon as we entered, I could tell from the look on Teeny's face that she had another surprise recipe to show us.

"Why are you smiling now?" I asked. "What have you been cooking up?"

Teeny rubbed her hands together. "Do you want me to tell you or do you want me to show you?"

"Just feed us whatever you've got as fast as possible," I said. "I think we all need to get the taste of what happened at Sudeer's house out of our mouths."

"You're right about that." Miss May walked to our booth in the back. Teeny and I followed. "I feel bad. Sudeer winds up a suspect in so many of these investigations. I understand why Kayla was upset."

I sighed. "Me too." I turned to Teeny. "OK I'm ready for my secret food now."

Teeny beckoned to Samuel the pimply-faced waiter, and he emerged with another silver platter. "Ladies. Today on the menu we have a delicious concoction born from the magnificent brain of our owner and head chef, Teeny."

Teeny beamed. "Thank you very much, Samuel. I like that word, magnificent. Well said."

Samuel placed the platter on the table and removed the silver top. "I trust you'll be flabbergasted by the taste experience you're about to enjoy. Please call for me if there's anything you need."

Miss May shook her head. "Such a weird kid. Reminds me of Germany."

I'd been so caught up in the case, I hadn't been missing Germany as acutely. But as soon as Miss May said his name, I felt the space of his absence. I sighed and looked fondly after the teenager. "He does remind me of Germany. But I think he's less weird. Germany is...from another planet."

Teeny handed each of us a fork and pushed the platter to our side of the table. I realized I hadn't even looked at the food yet. On the plate sat three enormous, golden-brown pancakes.

Miss May turned down the sides of her mouth, impressed. "Pancakes. They look fluffy and delicious. Did you use the extra buttermilk from the hush puppy recipe?"

"Of course I used the extra buttermilk. But that's not what makes these pancakes special. Cut into one and take a bite."

Miss May and I each stabbed a bite of pancake with a fork. As soon as I cut into the fluffy circle of goodness I saw the secret ingredient... "Is there macaroni and cheese in this pancake?"

Teeny laughed and slapped the table. "You got it. That's a macaroni and cheese pancake. Isn't it brilliant? Easy, too. I made my incredible, award-winning macaroni and cheese, then I put it in the pancake."

Miss May and I laughed. We each took a bite of pancake. The outside was crispy, which I loved. But the inside was filled with delicious, not-too-cheesy macaroni and cheese. Teeny had used elbows for the macaroni and each one gushed with the perfect amount of cheese when I bit into it. It was velvety and warm and so savory I felt like I was back in front of the fireplace at Miss May's. Teeny always cooked with love and it was apparent in every one of her dishes.

"How does it taste?" Teeny leaned forward.

"You know it's good," said Miss May.

Teeny snickered and took a bite of her own. "You're right. I know it's amazing. A Teeny recipe for the ages. Maybe I'll make a big stack and send them over to Sudeer's house as an apology."

Miss May shrugged. "Not a bad idea. Perhaps I should send a couple more pies as well."

"I'm glad Kayla had that receipt to prove Sudeer's innocence," I said. "Because the way he stammered back there... He seemed guilty. Or nervous or something."

Miss May nodded. "I suppose he was trying to prove his innocence without revealing the secret about the necklace he had bought. Poor guy. Seems like he's had a rough few weeks. He must feel so strange now that Beth is dead."

"Yeah, weirdly it made me feel even worse for Beth," I said. "I mean, yeah she was volatile and kind of mean, but it's clear that she suffered from mental illness and that manifested in lots of ways. I think she probably needed help and she didn't know where or how to get it."

"I think you're right," said Miss May. "She was definitely unpredictable. She lived a wild life and she was bold.

There's no telling how many people she might have offended."

"The more we learn about this case," said Teeny. "The more it reminds me of this delicious macaroni and cheese pancake. From the outside, everything appears normal. Just your standard pancake. But when you break into the middle, there's a whole secret ingredient hidden below the surface. Past the bottom, as Chelsea would say."

Miss May chuckled. "Well put, Teeny."

I took a big sip of water to wash down the pancake. "Who should we talk to next?"

"I've been thinking about that all morning," said Miss May. "There are a few leads we can pursue. We can talk to Beth's brothers to find out what else they know. They could be suspects in this. We can try to track down Lillian, the woman who gave the eulogy. Although she seemed just as erratic and unsettled as Beth. And then, of course, there's the question of this notebook."

Miss May pulled the marble notebook out of her purse and placed it on the table. "I stayed up late last night and read every entry."

My eyes widened. "You did? When were you going to share that information?"

"It's been a busy morning. Forgive me."

"OK. Sorry." I took another bite of pancake. I felt a little guilty for questioning Miss May's tactics, but the pancake made my bad feelings go away. *Aren't pancakes wonderful like that? If you ever need to forget your troubles, a short stack, a fork, and... OK, now I'm rambling.*

"So what did you learn?" asked Teeny.

"I thought there might be a code in there. Since all the entries are so mundane. When I started off reading the notebook, I assumed there had to be something more. But every time I turned the page, it was just another list of Beth's boring activities. So I went back to the list of people Beth thought wanted to kill her. I re-examined the suspects and their potential motives."

"They were all ridiculous," I said. "Miss May nodded her head. "I agree. But one name didn't have any motive listed beside it. It was flagged with a star and that's it."

I narrowed my eyes. "Oh yeah. Big Jim."

"He argued with Beth at the peach festival. He acted belligerent at Beth's funeral. Then he got into a public argument with Lillian," Miss May said. "Something was off about Big Jim and we need to find out what."

Teeny pulled the plate of pancakes close to her chest. "Can we go after we finish the pancakes?"

Miss May laughed. "Sure. I have a bad feeling we might need all our strength for this next confrontation."

19

ILLUSION OF TRUTH

We arrived at *Big Jim's Magic Emporium* around 2 pm that day. When we got there, Big Jim was locking up and hanging a "CLOSED" sign on the door. He was dressed in clothes just like what he wore to Beth's funeral. Tattered jeans, stained T-shirt.

He turned away from the door, spotted us and gave a little yelp of surprise. "Whoa, ladies. Those walking shoes must be expensive because I couldn't hear you coming at all. What's with the sneak attack?"

"Sorry," I said. "We didn't mean to scare you."

The magic shop was housed in a cute little cottage on the outskirts of town. It had a big, fancy sign that said "*Big Jim's Magic Emporium*," in bold letters. Even Big Jim, whose size matched his nickname, somehow seemed minuscule standing beneath the signage. "You ladies almost gave me my second heart attack. Not fun. What's up? Something tells me you're not here to purchase any of my books or novelty magic items. Although, Teeny, I think you'd make a great magician's assistant." Big Jim smirked flirtatiously.

"If I've told you once, I've told you eight hundred times...

I'm not going to be anyone's assistant." Teeny crossed her arms. "Stop asking me."

"OK. How are things with Big Dan, by the way?" Big Jim asked. Big Dan was the local mechanic, and Teeny's current crush. Even though she was unwilling to give their relationship any official labels.

Did Teeny have a thing for guys whose first name was Big?

Miss May and I lit up with identical grins at the mention of Big Dan and turned to Teeny. My aunt and I both loved Teeny's casual flirtationship with Big Dan. But I think we were equally delighted by Big Jim's overt pick-up attempts.

"Daniel is doing quite well. Thank you for asking."

"He might be able to fix a car, but I can make one disappear." Big Jim smiled.

Teeny shrugged. "Why would I want my car to disappear? I need my car to get around. It's very cute and practical. And Big Dan just gave me a great deal on replacing the belts."

"OK. I'm barking up the wrong tiny little tree. I get it. So what's going on?"

"Can we talk inside?" Miss May asked. "It's a sensitive subject."

Big Jim grumbled. "I was about to grab a burger and fries from *Ewing's Eats*."

"No milkshake?" Teeny asked. "What are you, a monster?"

"This won't take long," Miss May said.

The inside of Big Jim's magic shop was quaint and charming with a hint of strange. The room was a simple square with velvet maroon walls. Sturdy wood shelves displayed items for sale. There was a kit for pulling a rabbit out of a hat. There was an entire section dedicated to spells and incantations. There were dozens of trick card decks and instructional manuals on how to perform magic. Big Jim closed the door behind us as we entered.

"Welcome to the shop." He walked around the counter and stood beside the cash register. "Now, will you accuse me of murder already so I can get on with my day?"

Miss May grinned. "Our reputation precedes us."

"You've solved like three thousand murders in the past year and I love to read the *Pine Grove Gazette*, so yeah."

Miss May leaned on the counter. "You got into a big argument with Beth the day she died. And she accused you of wanting to kill her. Then you got into a fight with Lillian at Beth's funeral...it's not a becoming look."

"Very impolite," said Teeny. "And couldn't you have worn a suit or least something business casual?"

Big Jim sighed. "You're right. I should've dressed nicer. But I didn't even plan on going to the funeral that day. One second, I'm in my car, driving. Thinking about how poor crazy Beth had been murdered. The next minute, I'm standing in the parking lot watching the funeral from afar. I wanted to leave before anyone spotted me. I was about to get back into my car when Lillian started screaming."

Miss May straightened up and paced the floor of the magic shop. "You knew Beth?"

"She came into the shop from time to time. I've got tons of mystical tomes and talismans. All that stuff she was into... books from my store taught her the art. Beth was troubled, you know. Half the time she came in here, it was a normal transaction. The other half of the time, she'd come in and yell about how I wanted to ruin her life and discredit her magical powers. That's what Lillian thought of me — that I was out to besmirch Beth's name."

"Tell me more about that," said Miss May.

Jim picked at one of his teeth. "Ah I don't know. I never

really tried to discredit Beth, but... Well, one day I had a big crowd of people in here. They had all just come from a reading with Beth. I guess she was doing readings over at Salazar's for a while. These folks were gushing about some woman with true magical powers. She could see the future. She could speak to the dead. I tried to bite my tongue but I guess I wasn't hungry for tongue that day. Because I started blabbing about all the supplies that Beth buys here. I said she's not that special, blah, blah, blah. Then all those people left my shop and spread the word around town. 'Big Jim says Beth is a fraud.' Not my finest moment. I don't even know why I did it. But I did, and I can't take that back. Anyway, Lillian never forgave me. And I don't know how Beth felt about it. She kept coming into the shop. She had that creepy calm about her."

"Unless she was accusing you of premeditated murder, right?" Teeny asked.

"Yeah, that got her pretty worked up," Big Jim said.

I spotted a stool along the far wall. I pulled it over to the counter and took a seat. Miss May looked over at me with questioning eyes. "What? My feet hurt."

The truth? Jim's story felt heavy, and it made me want to sit down. *What was the problem with that, anyway? Sitting is great. Whoever invented sitting should get an award.*

"I think Sudeer's the guy you need to talk to," said Big Jim.

"Why should we talk to Sudeer?" Miss May asked. She already knew, of course, but it was always good to get different angles.

Big Jim's eyes widened. He leaned forward and he told us all about the Beth and Sudeer situation. Jim knew every detail about Beth stalking Sudeer. He seemed convinced that Sudeer had plenty of motive to commit the murder.

When Big Jim stopped talking, Miss May gave him a polite nod. "Thank you for the information. We'll take it into account. Did you share this intel with the police?"

Big Jim shrugged. "I tried to get in touch but the phone keeps ringing. I guess they're busy trying to solve this thing." Big Jim's phone rang. He checked the caller ID. "I'm sorry. I need to take this."

"No problem," said Miss May.

The phone rang again. Big Jim looked from Miss May, to Teeny, and then to me. "It's a private call."

Miss May nudged me off of my stool. "Alright. Thanks for your time."

I took one last look around Big Jim's magic shop as we left.

This mystery just kept getting more and more mysterious.

And I was starting to feel like finding this killer was going to be harder than pulling a rabbit out of a hat.

20

LOVE IS MAGIC

Miss May, Teeny, and I left Big Jim's and headed over to the *Brown Cow* for a cup of coffee. The little café had always been a source of comfort for me. I loved its soothing, homey decor. And Brian, the owner, always greeted us with a smile when we entered. That day was no different. Brian had a casual, Southern California charm and a quiet confidence that put me at ease.

"What's up, ladies? I presume you're here to take a break from your investigation?" Brian leaned forward. "You know I hear all the gossip. Do you have any questions for me?"

Miss May chuckled. "Sure. Has anyone come through the coffee shop talking about how they killed Beth?"

Brian looked up and to the left, thinking. "Now that I think of it... No. No one has come in and confessed to or talked about the murder loudly enough for me to hear. That would be awesome though. If I got that kind of information, would I be an official member of your team?"

Miss May grinned. "You already are. You supply the coffee."

I nodded aggressively. "She's right. Without coffee, none

of these investigations would've turned out well. I need caffeine for my karate chopping. And my walking. And my talking. And my karate kicking."

Brian pantomimed a few karate moves. His form was abysmal but it didn't seem worth mentioning. Instead, I pantomimed a few karate moves of my own. After a few seconds, Brian threw back his head and laughed. "I'm no match for you, Chelsea. You're pretty cool, do you know that?"

"She's the sweatiest cool girl I know," said Teeny. "Or maybe, the coolest sweaty girl I know?"

I hung my head. "Do we really need to talk about how sweaty I get? Can't I just be cool?"

"No worries," said Brian. "I already knew about the sweat. It's pretty public information."

We all laughed. Although I had once been more self-conscious about my insecurities, I'd loosened up since arriving in Pine Grove. Gained a little confidence. There were bigger problems in the world than my literal tendency to clam up. *Like murder, for instance.*

"Seriously though." Teeny leaned on the counter and lowered her voice. "Have you heard any gossip about the murder? Do you have any good leads?"

Brian groaned. "Man, I wish. I haven't overheard a truly interesting conversation in this coffee shop in days. Mostly people talk about their favorite TV shows or what they had for breakfast. Or, if I'm lucky, they spend most of their conversation gushing about how delicious my coffee is. But too few people spill anything juicy. They spill the creamer for their coffee, but not much else. That's why I'm always excited when you girls roll up to the shop."

Teeny grinned. "Excitement follows us like butter on a scone."

Brian wriggled his nose. "Is that an expression?"

Teeny nodded. "It's what they say in Britain."

"Teeny has been watching a lot of British television," said Miss May. "She hasn't quite gotten a handle on their expressions though."

"Blimey," said Teeny with an indignant frown. We all laughed again, and I took a moment to appreciate how everyone needs a little Teeny in their lives. *Or a big Teeny. A lot of Teeny?* Whatever. Teeny could always cheer me up, even when she was mad.

"Why don't you girls go take your table by the window?" Brian said. "I'll make your drinks and bring them over."

"Don't forget," said Teeny. "I like my coffee..."

"I know," said Brian. "Extra whipped cream and extra sprinkles."

Settled into our table by the window, we started talking about the case. We all agreed neither Big Jim nor Sudeer had been great leads. Sudeer had a strong, timestamped alibi. We felt bad for intruding on his family and we felt even worse that he had been stalked by Beth.

Big Jim's story about Beth and Lillian had been compelling, too. Miss May and Teeny were convinced he couldn't have had a hand in the murder but I wasn't so sure.

"I don't trust the guy," I said. "Something about him seems off."

Teeny dismissed me with a wave of her hand. "I agree. But that's just because he's a magician. You can never trust a magician. My mother taught me that and it's one of the smartest things she ever said."

Miss May looked confounded. "Your mother taught you not to trust magicians?"

"Oh yeah," said Teeny. "Back in the 70's I had a big magician phase. I dated three magicians in a row. Each one disappeared."

I laughed. "Good one."

"I'm serious," said Teeny. "They all vanished into thin air. One day, we're going to the movies and chatting and he's trying to convince me to be his sidekick. The next day he's gone forever."

"Magicians don't like to be tied down, I guess." I pulled my chair in and placed my elbows on the table. "But if you had all those experiences, why did your mom need to be the one who taught you to stop trusting magicians?"

"Ah, I had a blind spot. I was about to date magician number four. I found them so charming. But she pulled me aside and talked some sense into me."

"That's good," said Miss May. "Granny's a smart woman. And Chelsea, I think I agree with Teeny. Big Jim is just a weird magic nerd. But honestly, it sounded to me like he had a certain fondness for Beth. I feel bad for him."

"But she had that big star next to his name in the notebook. She thought Big Jim wanted to kill her."

"She thought everyone wanted to kill her," said Miss May.

"Yeah," said Teeny. "And who knows if we can even trust that notebook. Sure, Beth's name was on the cover. But what if it wasn't even hers? What if the killer had that notebook delivered to divert our attention?"

Both Miss May and I did a double-take at Teeny.

"That's an interesting theory," said Miss May.

"Yeah, it is," said Teeny. "I didn't even know I had that idea until it came out of my mouth but now that I've said it I feel smart."

"That's an elaborate distraction," I said. "And I don't

think we should discount the veracity of the book on a hunch. We need to verify the authenticity somehow."

Teeny furrowed her brow. "I agree. But how?"

"I have an idea," said Miss May. "But you're not going to like it."

Brian approached and placed a few drinks down on the table with a smile. "Enjoy, ladies."

He walked away and I looked at our drinks. Sure enough, Teeny's coffee was piled high with whipped cream and sprinkles. Usually, the sight of her drink would bring me a smile. But at that moment, I felt uneasy.

And no amount of sprinkles could fix it.

21

UP A TREE

"OK," I sighed, knowing exactly where Miss May was headed. "You want to find a way into Beth's house and find another sample of her handwriting to compare to the handwriting from the notebook."

"That's right." Miss May climbed into the front seat of Teeny's car and I jumped in the back. Teeny was already in the driver's seat, fixing her hair and straightening her sunglasses.

"That makes sense to me," I said. "But what I don't understand is how you think we're going to get inside Beth's house?"

Miss May shrugged. "Going to have to figure that out when the time comes. I've got a purse filled with pies so I can charm the brothers if necessary."

Teeny started the car. "Your purse is not filled with pies."

Miss May opened her purse and Teeny looked inside. "Fine. Your purse is filled with pies. But those are mini pies so they don't really count."

"A mini pie is a pie, Teeny."

"Ugh," Teeny said. "I guess you're right. And those pies look delicious. Can I have one?"

Miss May snapped her purse closed. "Sorry. We might need these where we're headed."

"I dunno," I said. "It's not like we're gonna show up and those creepy brothers are going to say, 'thank you for the pie please enter my home and review all my dead sister's written documents.'"

Miss May turned back and glared at me. "Chelsea. What's with the pessimism? When we need information, we get the information. That's how we work."

"You're right," I grumbled. "Consider my attitude adjusted. Let's do this."

Teeny slammed on the gas and sped out of town with a cheerful holler. I decided not to focus on my feelings of skepticism and instead focused on the feeling of the summer air pushing my hair off my forehead. It felt good and that was enough to salve my anxiety in the moment.

We pulled up to Beth's house in Blue Mountain to find that there were no cars in the driveway. "Looks like no one's home," said Miss May. She climbed out of the car and smoothed her pants with her palms. "Let's see what we can do here."

"Breaking and entering. Great," I said. "My favorite part of any investigation."

Teeny giggled. "I know you're being sarcastic but it really is my favorite part of these mysteries. I was born to burgle."

"You were not," said Miss May. "You were born to cook."

"I can be born for more than one thing! I'm not saying I'm a bad cook," said Teeny. "I'm just pointing out that I'm small and I step lightly and I can fit in tiny spaces."

"We might not even have to break into this place," I said.

"Maybe we could just wait for the brothers to come back. I'd rather avoid getting arrested today if possible."

Miss May rolled her eyes. "No one is getting arrested, Chelsea. Come on. Let's go around back."

Over the course of the next ten minutes, Teeny, Miss May, and I tried every door and window to the entire first floor of the house. Every single point of entry had been locked and the home seemed impenetrable. Then Teeny had an idea that made me feel queasy in my ears. *Don't know what I mean by that? Just wait 'til you hear the idea...*

Teeny pointed at a large oak tree off to the side of the house. "That's a beautiful tree, don't you girls think?"

Miss May and I shrugged. Teeny grinned. "Looks like it would be easy to climb for a healthy young woman. And that big branch reaches right onto the roof by the second floor. Now, call me crazy, but that third window over is cracked, isn't it?"

I groaned. "Please don't make me climb that tree."

"We're not making you do anything," said Miss May. "Justice is."

As a kid, I'd loved climbing trees. Then again, as a kid I had been rail thin, all elbows and knees. I had been a veritable tree-climbing machine. As an adult, I had the same elbows and knees I had had when I was a kid but they were surrounded by extra padding. Not ideal for lifting myself up and squeezing in between branches.

That's probably why it took me half an hour to get to the big branch that stretched onto the roof. Teeny had been right, the tree wasn't difficult to climb, even for me. There were plenty of footholds and I only scratched myself five or six times. But I overthought every moment of my climb. I second-guessed which branches to climb onto, which to hold onto for support, and where to place my feet.

After what felt like several decades trapped in an elevator, I finally popped off the big branch and onto the roof of Beth's house. I wiggled the window open wider, then looked back down at Teeny and Miss May. They each gave me a big thumbs up. Then I crawled inside, feeling victorious. That was the last positive thing that happened that day.

Even though I made it up the tree, our search of Beth's house did not go well. In fact, in many ways, it could not have gone worse.

Which is probably why I ended up spending the night in jail.

22

HANDWRITING ON THE WALL

I flopped from the roof of Beth's house into a dirty, cluttered bathroom. The place had a thick layer of grime on the counters. Water dripped from the shower head. Toothpaste had spilled near the sink and hardened.

"OK. Don't be judgmental, Chelsea," I muttered to myself. "But do get out of this place because it's disgusting and how could anyone live like this and oh my goodness gross gross gross."

Needless to say, I ran out of that bathroom as fast as my stubby little legs could take me. In the hallway, I ran straight into a bookshelf and knocked over seven vases. *Who keeps so many vases on a bookshelf? And how is it possible that they all smashed into a million pieces?*

I bent down to clean the glass, then realized how silly I was being. "Chelsea. Get a grip," I grumbled. "You can't clean that up it's going to take forever. You're here on a mission. Find a sample of Beth's handwriting and compare it to the notebook."

"Let us in." Miss May called from outside. I'd almost forgotten. Teeny and Miss May could help in the search.

Also, they had the notebook with them out there. Which we were going to need.

I opened the back door and let Teeny and Miss May in to the cluttered sunporch. "What was that crashing sound?" Miss May asked.

"I broke seven vases."

"How did you possibly manage that?" Miss May asked, incredulous.

"They were all in one spot."

Teeny threw up her hands. "Who keeps seven vases all in one place?"

I shook my head. "It was a bookshelf covered in vases. I suppose that makes it a vase shelf. I don't know. Let's start the search."

Once back inside, we fanned out to search efficiently. Miss May scoured the kitchen for handwriting samples. Teeny took the living room and I set off for the upstairs to find Beth's bedroom.

I could take a couple of minutes to tell you how gross and disgusting every single room in the house was, but that would feel rude. I didn't want to speak ill of the dead, or her abode, but man, Beth was not a clean person. Suffice it to say, every room in the house was at least as gross as that upstairs bathroom.

I'm talking grime upon grime upon grime. That kitchen... I would never eat out of the kitchen. OK. Sorry, rambling, being a little judgmental. Let's get back to the story.

I pushed the door to Beth's bedroom open with a creak. The creak reminded me that we were there on a secret mission. I needed to stay focused and not get distracted by how gross things were. Yes, Beth and her brothers lived like animals, but two of the animals might return home at any moment and be ready to attack. The situation was tense and I felt the suspense clenching at my lungs.

Have I mentioned I hate breaking and entering?

I couldn't see an inch of Beth's floors because the entire room was covered in clothing. Even the bed had clothes piled up on it, with just a little space remaining for someone to sleep. I spotted a desk on the far wall and crossed toward it. "OK. Handwriting, handwriting..." There were a few papers scattered on the desk but they all seemed to be forms and printouts from the Internet. There were a few ads for the local pizza place that Beth had printed for whatever reason. There were a few old copies of the *Pine Grove Gazette*, I'm sure the editor of the local paper Liz would've been happy to know. But no handwriting.

"I guess people don't write by hand as much as they used to," I said, to no one. I considered this. I personally wrote things by hand all the time. At the bakeshop, it was always necessary to jot down notes to Miss May or alter recipes, and I often hand-scrawled customer receipts. But outside of that context I barely used handwriting at all.

I moved a few more papers aside and uncovered a clunky old laptop. I picked up the computer and I swear it was so heavy it made my arms tired.

I opened the ancient laptop and it prompted me for a password. I looked around, trying to guess what Beth's password might be. *DirtyBedroom? GrossHouse 123?* I turned the laptop upside down to see if the password been taped to the bottom and the entire screen detached from the keyboard. I cringed. My visit to Beth's house had really taken breaking and entering to a whole new level, especially where the 'breaking' part was concerned. I did my best to sandwich the laptop back together, gave a deep sigh and exited.

Back downstairs, it seemed that Teeny and Miss May

hadn't had much more luck. Miss May was digging through a kitchen drawer with a ginger touch. Teeny was beside her, apparently having given up on the living room.

"Find anything?"

Miss May looked up, exasperated. "There's not a stitch of handwriting in this entire home. Did you have any luck?"

I shook my head. "No. But I destroyed the victim's computer."

Miss May rubbed her forehead. "That's disappointing."

Teeny grabbed an envelope from a pile of papers on the kitchen counter. "One second. What's this?" She handed the envelope to Miss May. "It's from *Five Pines*, the mental institution. There's a past-due sticker stamped on top."

Miss May looked from Teeny and then over to me. "Maybe that rumor about Beth being institutionalized was more than a rumor."

I shrugged. "There's one good way to find out."

Miss May opened the envelope and pulled the letter out from inside. Her eyes widened. "Oh my goodness. Beth has been in and out of *Five Pines* several times in the past couple years. Looks like she was in there a week before she died. And she owes a lot of money. Well, owed. I guess her brothers owe it now..."

Teeny and I crowded around Miss May to get a better look at the document. Teeny covered her mouth. "Goodness! That is a lot of money!"

I winced. "Yes it is."

Miss May slid the paper back in the envelope and returned the envelope to its place on the kitchen counter. "I wonder if her murder had something to do with *Five Pines*. I know mental health facilities can be helpful to some people, but *Five Pines* doesn't have a great reputation."

"What do you mean?" I asked.

Miss May spoke slowly. "There've been reports of poor conditions. Violent patients. Irresponsible orderlies...I don't think it's a very nice place to live."

"Maybe we should go there," I said.

"You're not going anywhere until you tell me what you're doing in my home."

We spun around to face the back door. There stood Jonathan, Beth's chubby little bald brother. And he was holding a gun.

23

GUNNING FOR TROUBLE

Let's pick up where we left off.

With me, Teeny, and Miss May standing in the kitchen and Jonathan pointing a gun at us.

Honestly, my first thought was that Jonathan was the killer. Our mysteries had concluded before with us being threatened at gunpoint.

But then I thought, it would be all too easy if the killer just gave himself up like that. It didn't make sense. I glanced over at Miss May. Her hands were up and her face was calm. I could tell she didn't think Jonathan was the killer either.

"Hi Jonathan," said Miss May. "I'm going to be very honest with you now, OK?"

Jonathan's hand was trembling. His gun wobbled as his arms shook. "OK. Talk."

"You know this already but Teeny, Chelsea, and I broke into the home you share with your sister. Yes. We're not here to hurt anyone or to steal anything. As I'm sure you're aware, we are amateur detectives. When something goes wrong in Pine Grove, we investigate."

"Everybody knows that."

"Our sole focus right now is to find the person who killed your sister to make sure they go to jail for a long time for what they did. Under normal circumstances, we wouldn't have broken in here. Of course. But there's a killer on the loose right now. And we thought this home may contain evidence that would help us find that person."

Jonathan clasped his free hand around the gun so both hands were now clutching the weapon.

"Why are we telling him we broke in?!" said Teeny.

"Because it's true," said Miss May. "Obviously we don't live here."

Teeny shook her head and looked at Jonathan. "That's not true. You can put the gun down because she lied. We didn't break in. Your other brother was home when we got here and he let us in. And he's still here. Upstairs somewhere. You should go find him."

"I'm not an idiot. Michael isn't home."

Teeny looked over at Miss May as if to suggest it was worth a try. But even I, the queen of bad lies, knew Teeny really flubbed that lie. Then again, I hadn't said a single word since the man with the gun showed up, so I wasn't really helping either.

"You're intruders. I don't care why you say you're here. You broke the law and I'm calling the police."

Miss May hung her head. "I know you want justice. Calling the police is not your best bet. We've solved more murders than our entire town's police force combined."

Jonathan swallowed. I could tell Miss May's logic was working on him. His head wavered from side to side. Then he snapped back to attention. "No. I don't care what you say. The police would never have come into a home without asking. They would need a warrant and they would do things the right way."

Teeny scoffed. "The police are fools. We don't have the resources they have, but what we do have is intelligence and smarts. We get it done, wrap it up, case closed, Bob's your uncle."

"What? Who's Bob?" Jonathan furrowed his brow.

"It's a British expression," said Miss May. "Don't ask." Miss May took a small step toward Jonathan. "Please lower the gun? This doesn't need to turn violent."

Jonathan maintained his wobbly grip on the gun. "Stay away from me. I said I'm calling the police."

Miss May retreated back a step. "Alright. Call the police."

The illustrious Detective Wayne Hudson arrived about fifteen minutes later in his unmarked car. He entered the kitchen to find me, Teeny, and Miss May still held at gunpoint by Jonathan. But Jonathan relaxed when Wayne entered and lowered the gun. Then, Wayne listened to Jonathan's entire story and refused to let us butt in, even when Jonathan was clearly exaggerating or making us look bad.

"Thank you for the information," said Wayne when Jonathan had stopped speaking. "These three know better than to break into the home of a stranger. I mean, any American citizen knows better. There are laws."

"He pulled a gun on us!" Teeny said.

"Technically, you broke into his home...so his actions count as self-defense," Wayne said. "Although, Jonathan, please be careful with that thing."

"I'm always careful," Jonathan responded. "Even when there are crazy people marauding around my house."

"We're not marauding, there's a killer and—" I started.

"And that's just another reason not to break into someone's home. People want to feel safe right now, not under threat."

Jonathan nodded. "Exactly. My sister was just killed. You think I want to find intruders snooping around her belongings?"

"You're right," said Miss May. "That's our bad. But I'm wondering, Wayne, why are you even here? We're in Blue Mountain, not Pine Grove."

"Pine Grove police patrol most of Blue Mountain. There's fewer than a thousand residents in this town so we handle it for the county. It's usually an easy beat."

Teeny crossed her arms. "I doubt anything is easy for the Pine Grove Police Department. You guys haven't solved a single crime in the past year."

"I'm solving one right now, Teeny," said Wayne. "You three are coming down to the station. I'm booking you for the night for breaking and entering."

Jonathan turned to Wayne. "You are?"

Wayne nodded. "That's right."

Jonathan nodded, satisfied. "Good."

Teeny's eyes widened. "Hold on. I'm sorry. I take it back. Wayne. Detective Hudson. Please. Don't make me spend the night in jail. Me and May are too old. We'll freeze to death. We're ancient. I'm a hundred and she's a hundred and nine. You can't send the elderly to jail like that. It's unconscionable."

"Why do I have to be hundred and nine?" Miss May asked.

"You're older than me."

"No I'm not, Teeny," said Miss May.

"Listen, girls. I understand what you're saying," Wayne said. "Even though, Teeny, you've told me a number of times that you're thirty-five and not to call you old." Teeny harrumphed. Wayne ignored her and continued, "You know

I like you both. But I need to book someone for this for the night."

All eyes turned to me. I groaned. "Why does my youth make me a better candidate for jail? If anything, age and wisdom should make a person better suited for that kind of hardship."

"So you want your aunt or Teeny to go in your place?" Wayne said, with what I swear was a hint of a smirk.

I sighed and held out my hands for Wayne to cuff me. Although I'd broken many laws and snooped around many crime scenes, that night was my very first time being arrested. Thankfully, Wayne spared me the cuffs.

"I'm not going to shackle you, Chelsea. Unless you resist."

I looked up at Wayne, and that was a mistake. His blue-green, green-blue, whatever-color-combo eyes seemed to sparkle mischievously. *Was Wayne...flirt-arresting me?*

"Chelsea?" Wayne said, clearing his throat.

I snapped back to reality. "I'm not going to resist."

Wayne turned to Jonathan. "Does this arrangement work for you, sir? Little unorthodox but we're a small-town department. Frankly, we barely have enough jail cells to accommodate Chelsea. And I can guarantee you, these two older women meant no harm. Chelsea didn't either, but I understand, they did commit a crime. That's why I'm going to book the young one for a night. You're going through a lot right now so you can decide over the next few days if you'd like to press charges."

"You better believe I'm pressing charges," said Jonathan. "Against all three of you. I don't care who spends the night in jail."

"OK," said Wayne. "You just let me know."

Wayne spent a few minutes writing up a report then we

left. Miss May and Teeny in the convertible and me in the back of Wayne's unmarked car.

Chief Sunshine Flanagan, my de facto archenemy on the force, set bail for $5000. That was high, in my opinion. And it wasn't something Miss May or Teeny could afford, at least not on short notice. So I spent my first ever night in jail.

And it was far more eventful than I could have ever expected.

24

I KNOW WHY THE JAILBIRD SINGS

Jail cells are not cozy. There's no other way to say it. The walls were bare and concrete. Metal bars never warmed anyone's heart. And even in a small town like Pine Grove, the jail cell in the back of the police department smelled a little moldy and unattended.

Still, I wasn't too freaked out as Hercules closed the door and locked me in. Despite the odor, and the cold, barren surroundings, I felt calm and almost at home. *Weird, I know.* But throughout the course of our investigations, a few of my loved ones, including KP and my Aunt DeeDee, had been locked up in that cell. And somehow, thinking of them in this same cell put me at ease. I even smiled as I thought about KP's purported love of jail food — "all potatoes, all the time!" I was sort of looking forward to having a jail meal...regardless of how the potatoes were prepared.

You really can't go wrong with a potato.

OK, so the decor wasn't cozy. The temperature was frigid. The vibe was sterile. But, I was hopeful that I wouldn't be in jail for long. My friends and family hadn't been held for too long. I called out to the skinny young Deputy Hercules as he padded back toward the main area of the police department. "Hercules!"

He turned back. "What's up, Chelsea? Are you OK? Do you need something? Again… Really sorry about this."

Hercules had been apologizing profusely ever since I had arrived at the station a few hours earlier. His behavior was a stark contrast to Chief Flanagan's — she had treated me like she'd witnessed me setting Town Hall on fire or stealing canes from the elderly.

"You're fine, Hercules. No need to apologize. I'm sure I'll get out of here soon. I was just wondering… This place is a bit bleak. Do you have a blanket or something? I'd love to spruce it up."

Hercules smiled. "I always forget you used to be a famous interior designer in New York City."

I shook my head. "Not famous."

"I'll see what I can…" Hercules stopped speaking in the middle of his sentence and widened his eyes. "Chief. Hi. What's going on?"

Chief Flanagan stormed down the hall toward my cell. Flanagan was undeniably glamorous. Her current riled state only added to her movie star quality. Her long red hair swished like a cape in time with her strides. Her bright eyes were sharp and focused.

A wild-eyed woman, hands cuffed behind her, walked a few steps in front of Flanagan.

"We got a second intake, Hercules. She's spending the night. Maybe more."

The woman cackled and licked her lips. She had a faraway look in her eyes. "Spending the night. I love spending the night in jail. We love it so much. Me and her and she and me. We won't hurt anyone. We'll try not to. You never know what might happen in the night." The woman laughed.

I gulped. *This was going to be my cellmate?*

"You want to put her in this cell?" Hercules asked. "With Chelsea?"

"Not ideal," said Flanagan. "But we're using the second cell for overflow storage, remember? There's no room so we don't have a choice."

I put my hands on the bars. "You could let me out. Over-crowding in jails is a problem. I'd be happy to solve it."

Flanagan glared at me. "Not an option."

Flanagan opened the door to my cell and shoved the manic woman inside. Then Flanagan made a sharp turn toward Hercules. "Deputy. Back to your desk. Follow me."

Flanagan charged away and Hercules followed on her heels like a little dog. My heart plummeted as I watched them go. I muttered something about my blanket but Hercules didn't hear me.

"You're my cellmate. Checkmate. Do you play chess? I love all sorts of games. So does she."

I turned to my new cellmate and tried to give her the benefit of the doubt in spite of her dramatic entrance. Maybe we could get along. Maybe we could even bond over our shared jail experience.

I scanned the woman from head to toe. She was wearing an extreme oversized dress. Her hair was greasy and matted. She had a hospital band on her wrist. It had five little tiny pine trees on it, which made me assume that this woman had been in *Five Pines* recently. From the way the woman seem to be talking to herself, I assumed she might suffer from schizophrenia. I felt bad for her. Mental health problems were no joke. Even if she heard voices or felt dissociated from reality, she was still a human being, struggling through something unimaginably hard. Everyone carried around her own handful of demons, but this woman seemed to have a whole satchel of demons. I could empathize with her.

But I also felt scared of her. *What had this woman done to end up in jail? And would she be a danger to me?*

"Hi. How are you? I mean, you're in jail, so probably not great, right? I would offer you a pie to help ease the transition but the cops confiscated all my baked goods." I chuckled awkwardly. The woman just stared at me, then turned her back and sat on the stiff bench-bed across the cell from me.

So much for bonding...

We stayed like that, sitting in silence for a long time. Probably a couple of hours, well past midnight. Neither of us seemed inclined to sleep or speak. Then, out of the blue, the woman started talking again — continuing the conversation from earlier as if no time had passed.

"I said I love playing games. We both do. And so does she." The woman cocked her head and gave me a plastic smile.

I almost jumped out of my skin when the woman spoke. "Games are fun, yeah. Uh, I'm Chelsea, by the way. What's your name?"

"Call me Jasmine. Everyone calls me Jasmine, even though it's not my name." Jasmine twirled and sang a little song. She stopped in the middle of the song and looked back at me. "Such a pleasure to meet you. The pleasure is all ours. I love living in big white houses. I spend way too long in the big brick scary building. This is nice compared to where I was."

I swallowed. "Oh? Where were you before this?" *Pretty*

sure I knew the answer, but I had to ask.

Jasmine held up her wrist. "*Five Pines.* Not *Four Pines*. Not *Three Pines*. *Five Pines* is the number of pines they use to indicate a mental institution. I don't know why it's *Five Pines*. There are hardly any trees. At least no trees that I could see from my tiny window."

I knew that Beth had spent time at *Five Pines,* and I wondered if Jasmine might have information about Beth that could help us solve the case. *I don't want to say that ending up in jail with Jasmine struck me as a lucky break*. But I was curious and hopeful.

Could Jasmine lead us to the killer?

If I was going to find anything out, I knew I would have to tread lightly so I chose my next words with careful precision. "I've heard about *Five Pines*. I'm glad you like it here better."

"So much better. One million times better." Jasmine stared off into space as she spoke.

"I had a friend who was there. And the staff wouldn't even let me visit her. Maybe you knew her... Beth?"

Jasmine's eyes widened and she stumbled back a few steps. "You knew Beth? Yes, I knew Beth. We all knew each other. Beth's the reason I'm here. That red-haired lady, the angry one? The one that I heard someone call Sunshine? Sunshine thinks I killed Beth. I didn't kill Beth. I was discharged the day Beth died but that doesn't make me guilty. Discharge does not make you guilty. It makes you free. It makes you free unless people think it makes you guilty. And then you end up in jail. And then maybe you end up back in *Five Pines*. I don't want to go back there. I didn't kill Beth, her crazy roommate did. At least that's what I think. Roommates often kill each other. I won't kill you, even though you're my roommate. Not unless you make me very, very angry."

My fingertips and scalp started to tingle as soon as Jasmine casually mentioned the possibility of murdering me. I tried to ignore the pins and needles in my extremities and focus on the case. "I'm sorry. Did you say Beth was killed by her roommate at *Five Pines*?"

"That's my theory. That's my working theory. And I love to work. People think that I've never liked to work but I had a lemonade stand when I was ten and it went so well I bought myself extra lemons for the next day. When life gives you lemons, buy extra lemons with the lemon money you make from the lemonade stand."

"Do you know the name of Beth's roommate?"

"Of course. I was the mayor of that place. I was very careful with my political moves. That's how I got to be the mayor."

"Thomas." I turned. There stood Chief Flanagan, outside the bars of the cell, arms crossed. "Stop hassling your cellmate."

"I wasn't—"

"Doesn't matter. You're going home." Flanagan opened the cell door and pulled me out by my wrist. I stammered. "I don't understand. Why am I getting out?"

"You made bail."

"Five thousand dollars? How?"

Flanagan shrugged. "Don't know. Don't care. I'm sure you'll find out soon enough."

I followed Flanagan down the hall, toward the main area of the police station. My mind flooded with questions.

Who had paid my bill? Why had they done it? And could Jasmine have been right about the killer?

As I walked out of the cell, I glanced back. I was happy to be going home, but I couldn't shake the feeling that I might have been seconds away from learning the name of a murderer...

25

FREEBIRD

I exited the police department into the darkness of the wee morning hours to find Miss May and Teeny standing in the parking lot, leaning against the VW bus.

I laughed as waves of relief and disbelief washed over me. "You two are unbelievable. You paid five grand to get me out of jail?"

"It wasn't all us," said Miss May. "We had a little help." Miss May walked around the side of the VW bus and gestured toward the road where at that precise moment, a parade of cars slowly rolled by the police department. Each car flashed its light and honked its horn. I recognized a lot of familiar faces from Pine Grove. All these people, driving by in the middle of the night, just to support me...

I wiped my eyes with my shirt sleeves. *Yeah, yeah, I immediately started to cry.* "Everyone in town..." I said, trying not to devolve into full-on ugly sobs.

Teeny patted me on the shoulder. "They heard about the crazy bail and they chipped in. Five dollars here, a hundred there... We hit five thousand and we barely had to try." I spotted KP driving by in his pickup truck. He stuck his head out the window with a smile. "How'd you like my cell, girly? Hope you got some potatoes while you were in there."

"I didn't," I called back.

"Why?"

I laughed. "Got in too late, got out too early."

"Ah, too bad," KP grumbled, and drove away.

The stream of slow moving cars lasted for about five minutes. Brian from the *Brown Cow* drove by with his husband, Mr. Brian, in a cute little sedan. Liz, the editor of the *Gazette*, rode by on her bicycle, dinging the bell. Tom Gigley cruised by in his antique Mercedes, blasting one of his own songs from the stereo. Tears casually rolled down my cheeks for the whole procession. Then, the cars were gone almost as fast as they had arrived. I wrapped Miss May and Teeny up in a big hug. "I'm so glad I moved home. It's worth going to jail just to see how kind people can be."

"Silver lining." Miss May dabbed at her own eyes. My aunt wasn't a big crier, but even she was susceptible to the poignancy of extreme kindness.

"Why are we crying?" asked Teeny, who was also crying.

"Because this was a beautiful gesture," I said. "And that makes me cry."

I stepped out of the hug and wiped my eyes again. *Crying time, over.* We needed to get down to business. "Pine Grove is such a wonderful community. That's why we need to find the killer. I'm sick of people treating the citizens of Pine Grove like they're dispensable. No one can murder our friends and neighbors and get away with it."

"Yeah. Even if the people who die are awful it's not right," Teeny said.

"So what do we do now?" I asked.

A gruff man cleared his throat from a few feet behind us. We turned. Wayne stood at the entry to the police department with an impatient look on his face. "I suggest you girls hit the road. Flanagan is on a rampage. You didn't hear it from me." Wayne disappeared back into the police department. He took big, long strides. The longest strides I had ever seen anyone take. Like he had Gumby legs. He was tall, that was probably why.

"Nice caboose on that kid," said Teeny.

Miss May laughed. "Get in the car, ladies. We should get out of here." On the ride back over to Teeny's house, I told Miss May and Teeny all about what had happened in jail.

Neither of them had ever heard of Jasmine before but they were both stunned by what Jasmine had told me. And they were irate at Chief Flanagan for treating me in such a harsh manner. I tried to say that I'd felt pretty comfortable in jail, considering it was jail, but Teeny and Miss May were still all fluffed up about Flanagan's attitude.

Half an hour later, the three of us were getting ready for bed in Teeny's pastel pink bathroom, and we were still talking about the case. "Wayne seemed serious back at the station," I said. "I mean, he always seems kind of serious. But I think this time, Flanagan isn't messing around. She's determined to stop us and it seems to me like that's more important to her than solving the case. I mean, she already arrested someone. And I really don't think Jasmine is guilty. I don't know what comes next."

Teeny spoke as she brushed her teeth. White foam bubbled from her mouth. "Well we're not going to stop pursuing the case. But we need to stay out of her way while we investigate."

Miss May brushed back her hair. "So we'll keep investigating but we won't break any more laws."

Teeny and I both turned to face Miss May. "I'm serious," said Miss May. "We can solve a murder without breaking laws. We should always strive to abide by the law while we investigate, anyway. This will be a fun challenge."

Teeny shook her head. "That is absurd, May. Sometimes you need to break the law to set things right. Even Mr. Flowers breaks laws and he has three degrees from Oxford in horticulture and he drinks tea with his pinky up. Jenna doesn't drink tea with her pinky up because she's low-born. She thinks it's silly how Mr. Flowers drinks tea. But she does not think it's silly that he sometimes breaks laws to solve murder mysteries. That's par for the course."

Miss May turned up her palm. "I don't think we have much of a choice. My little Chelsea is not going to spend one more night in jail. I don't care how good the potatoes are."

"I heard they're delicious," said Teeny. "One time I called the cook over there to try and get the recipe. She knew it was my voice and she wouldn't tell me anything. So frustrating to have such an adorable and recognizable voice in this town."

"Let me remind you, I did not even get to sample the potatoes," I said.

"Oh, sorry, did we bail you out too soon?" Teeny asked.

"No!" I splashed some water on my face, the lazy woman's face-washing method, and looked back over at Miss May. "So what are we gonna do next that doesn't break any laws? Any ideas?"

Miss May shrugged. "It's obvious, isn't it?"

Teeny and I made eye contact in the mirror. It wasn't

obvious to me and I don't think was obvious to Teeny either.

"I don't think it's obvious to either of us," I said. "Tell us."

Miss May tied her hair back in a loose ponytail. "We need to go to *Five Pines*. We need to see what we can learn about Beth's time there. And we need to talk to that murderous roommate."

26

NOT THREE PINES, NOT FOUR PINES

Five Pines was a turn-of-the-century brick building up on a hill overlooking Pine Grove. After Jasmine's description of the place, I was expecting something austere and institutional, but she'd been all wrong about the aesthetics of her former abode.

The grounds were covered, and I mean covered, in pine trees. Five pines was a wild understatement. More like, five thousand pines. The building itself was beautiful, and we pulled up on a beautiful day. It felt more like we were showing up for a picnic at a manor than pulling up to a mental health facility.

We arrived at around nine in the morning. It was a 70° day. The sky was blue with cotton candy clouds. We parked off to the side of the building and climbed out of Teeny's convertible. I looked around. "Is it just me... Or is this place gorgeous?"

Miss May nodded. "It's lovely. Before it was a mental hospital, it was home to one of Pine Grove's wealthiest citizens. I think he was a logging millionaire in the late 1800's. Rumor is, he built this place for his wife and his wife was mentally ill. People say that after she died, he turned the home into a mental hospital to help others like her through their struggles."

"That's a good husband," said Teeny. "I hope my husband opens a mental hospital after I die. So romantic."

I shrugged. "I guess. But you're not mentally ill. Or married."

Teeny shrugged. "A girl can dream."

I chuckled. "You want Big Dan to open a mental hospital in your honor?"

Teeny huffed and blushed. "I didn't say that."

Miss May started up a flight of concrete stairs toward the main entrance.

Teeny and I followed. "You really think they're just going to tell us who Beth's roommate was?" Teeny called up to Miss May.

"Sure," said Miss May. "We'll use our wits and our charm. We'll loosen them up with some pie."

Inwardly, I worried that the residents of Pine Grove were beginning to catch on to Miss May's "pies-as-bribes-for-information" routine, but I didn't say it out loud. Even if people knew the schtick, it was still hard to resist fresh, homemade pie.

We took the elevator to the third floor and piled out into a small waiting room. A gaunt, seven-foot-tall man eerily stood behind the counter, typing on a computer. He was easily the tallest man I had ever seen in real life. Any comforting feelings I'd felt outside in the picturesque parking lot were replaced by dread at the sight of the skeletal giant at the reception desk. He spoke without looking up from his computer. His voice was deep and booming which, in my opinion, was the scariest type of voice he could have had. "Sign into the guestbook. List the name and room number of patient with whom you'd like to visit. Provide your government ID's. Thank you."

"Actually, we're not here to visit a patient," Miss May said.

"You're not here to visit me, either," said the skinny man. "So why are you here?"

The man looked up from his screen, and somehow his gaze was even more unsettling than his other features. He had pale blue eyes like a Siberian Husky. They were flat and emotionless.

The kind of eyes that take you by surprise, no matter how well you know them.

Miss May stammered. "As it happens, I believe we are here to visit you." Miss May pulled an individual-sized peach pie from her purse. "Do you like pie?"

The man leaned over and sniffed the pie. "I'm allergic to peaches."

Miss May replaced the pie in her purse and pulled out an apple pie. Once again, the man looked over. "I don't like apple pie. Generally, pies disgust me. They have crust so you think you can pick them up and eat them like a slice of pizza. But if you pick up a slice of pie you end up with pie all down your front and on your pants. It's unsanitary and I don't like it. Please put the pie away."

Miss May looked over at me. I shrugged. It seemed that without pie we would have to rely solely on our wits if we were going to get any information from the deep-voiced beanstalk.

"Why are you trying to bribe me with pie?" *I knew people were onto the pie bribes.*

Teeny snickered. "Bribe. Bribe is a harsh word. We are just here to trade pie for information. That's not a big deal.

That's small town living at its finest. We bring you a pie and you tell us what we need to know."

The skinny man narrowed his eyes. "You want information about Beth."

Miss May nodded. "That's right. We were friends of Beth's."

"Beth didn't have a lot of friends. And the three of you are not her type. Try the truth."

Miss May looked from me over to Teeny. Teeny smiled her big, nervous smile. Not very helpful but extremely cute. "I'm smiling but it doesn't seem to be charming him," Teeny said through gritted teeth.

Miss May turned back to the man. "I love to tell the truth. The truth is that we are amateur detectives. We want to solve the case of Beth's murder and we think you have information that could prove useful in our investigation. You are correct about the pie. I was trying to use it to endear myself to you in hopes that you provide the information we need."

"But I hate pie."

"Yes, you mentioned," Miss May said. "An unexpected obstacle but I still think the four of us can work together."

"I can't tell you anything. That's the law. I don't like pie but I love the law. Before I worked here, I studied to be a lawyer but I was too tall for that."

"There's no height limit for lawyers," said Teeny. "I know, because I used to think I was too short to be a lawyer."

"She's right," Miss May said. "I know, because I actually used to be a lawyer."

"The other lawyers picked on me. They called me the world's tallest lawyer. They tried to climb me like a tree. I dropped out of law school after three months. The hardest three months of my life. The people here, at this institution?

They don't judge me. They all have freakish abnormalities, just like me."

"I'm glad you found sufficient comfort among other people who understand you," I said. "That's important in life. Comfort."

"You're right. And it's hard for me to be comfortable. Especially when people try to climb you like a tree. I also hate when people ask me if I play basketball. Do I look like I play basketball?"

"Kind of," said Teeny. She clasped her hands over her mouth. "Sorry. No. You don't. Was the correct answer no?"

"I'm not athletic. I believe that's clear for all to see despite my height. For instance, look closely at the hunch of my spine. Not the spine of a 'baller.'"

"Anyway..." Miss May leaned on the counter. "Is there any chance you can help us out? All we want to know is who Beth's roommate was..."

"The records are sealed. And so is my mouth. I can't tell you anything and I won't. Also, I would not have told you anything even if I did like pie. I would have eaten the pie and then refused to help. Because I'm a man of honor."

Miss May looked into the man's eyes for ten seconds straight. He did not flinch. I'm pretty sure he didn't even blink. Finally, she turned back to me and Teeny. "OK. Let's get out of here."

We gave them in a polite nod and headed down the hall, back toward the elevator. "What are we going to do now?" I asked.

Miss May entered the elevator and pressed the floor marked with a B. She looked at me with a mischievous glimmer in her eye. "We're going to the record room."

Teeny and I groaned and said in perfect unison, "So much for not breaking the law."

27

GOING DOWN

DING. BING. The elevator doors opened into a narrow, cement hall. Water dripped from an unknown source. Little rodent footsteps scurried in the walls. The place smelled like an unpleasant mix of terror and mold. I swallowed and the sound echoed off the walls.

"Why are we down here?" I whispered.

"It's the basement. I'm assuming this is where they keep the records." Miss May looked around. "It's awful dark though."

Teeny flipped a switch on the wall. A row of yellow light bulbs lit up one by one, from the spot where we stood all the way down to the other end of the hall. It was very cinematic.

Doors lined the hallway. There were no windows on the doors and we couldn't see inside the rooms. "Do you think they used to keep patients down here?" I tried one of the door knobs and it was locked. "I know the story about how this place was started is sweet but a lot of mental institutions have checkered pasts. I heard about one place where they tested patients by pulling their teeth right out of their—"

Teeny held up her hand. "Enough. That's enough. That is not a *Jenna and Mr. Flowers*-approved conversation. I don't want to think about anything more atrocious than the way this place smells. It does not smell good."

"Fair," I said. I turned to Miss May. "So what now?"

Miss May shrugged. "We try every door. We'll find something. And if we're lucky, one of these rooms will house the hospital records."

We were lucky. The first door I tried opened to a small room stacked with papers, folders and filing cabinets. I picked up one of the folders. It was dated from the year 1959. "They don't throw anything away in this place."

"Is there any organizational system in here, I wonder?" Miss May opened the drawer in a filing cabinet. "This cabinet is alphabetical, kind of. But it's only A through G."

Someone whistled a happy tune from out in the hall. Miss May, Teeny, and I froze. "Who's that?" Teeny squeaked. "I'm scared. This is not how I want to die."

"No one is going to kill us, Teeny." Miss May looked at the crack in the door. "I don't see anyone."

The whistling continued. "Look closer." I joined Miss May at the door. "Someone is down in this basement. Whistling."

"Unless it's a ghost whistle," Teeny gasped.

At that moment, the tall, skinny man from upstairs strolled by, eating a sandwich. He had little white headphones in his ears and he was bopping his head along to music. Miss May and I stumbled back into the records room, shocked.

Teeny stepped toward us. "What? What was it? Did you see a ghost?"

"It was the skinny giant." I peeked back outside and the man was gone. "He was eating a sandwich."

Teeny gasped. "Who would eat down here? Disgusting."

"There must be a break room down in the basement." Miss May closed the door. The latch did not make a noise as the door shut. "We better move quick. We're in trouble if that guy finds us."

Teeny pointed at another filing cabinet, across the room from the one Miss May had opened earlier. "Chelsea. Check in there."

I popped open the first drawer. My eyes widened. "I think this is it. H through Z. Let's see. Jenkins... Beth Jenkins... Is she in here?"

"Look carefully," said Miss May. "Some of the folders stick together. Don't miss any."

I winced. Miss May was right. Several of the folders had been stuck together. I tried to ignore it but now that she had said it out loud I felt queasy. What kind of ooze had glued these ancient papers to themselves? "This place doesn't take any pride in record-keeping," I said.

"It's a second-rate institution," said Miss May. "Even third or fourth."

"I found it." I pulled out a folder labeled Jenkins, Beth. "This is the file."

"What's it say?" Teeny asked.

"Basic stuff. These are the results from her physical. She was in good health so we know there was no underlying cause for her death."

"What room was she in? Who was her roommate?"

I flipped the page. And there was the information we wanted. I couldn't believe my eyes. "Oh my goodness," I said.

"What?" Teeny whispered so loud it was almost a shriek. "Tell us what you found."

"Beth's roommate was Lillian Edwards!"

Miss May blinked fast a few times. "The woman who gave Beth's eulogy? How could that be?"

I shrugged. "I'm not sure. But according to these records, Lillian is still a patient at this hospital. And she's staying in room 408."

28

UPSTAIRS, DOWNSTAIRS

Neither me, nor Teeny, nor Miss May wanted to ride the elevator back up from the basement. We'd felt trapped in the creepy elevator earlier, so we wanted to find a different exit. As soon as the skinny giant was out of earshot, we slipped into the hall and looked for an alternate way out.

"There's probably an exit down here somewhere," I said. "We just have to look."

Miss May nodded. "I agree. You go first."

She gave me a little nudge and I headed down the hall.

Drip. Drip. Drip.

Water seemed to ooze from every ceiling crack, every rusty pipe in sight. I needed to get out of there. I walked with cautious determination. I craned my neck to peer into some of the doors we passed, but they were all unmarked, windowless, and creepy.

"This basement is a disgrace," said Teeny. "I would never send someone I love to to be a patient at this place. What's in all these other rooms? Dead bodies, probably."

Miss May sighed. "Teeny. No. I'm sure it's just more

records and...I don't know. There are a lot of doors in this hallway."

Teeny looked around with wide eyes. "I dunno. I think it's a bunch of dead bodies. I bet those sickos in the doctor coats are experimenting on people then killing 'em and putting 'em down here like the Parisian catacombs."

"Alright. Enough. Please. I don't think the basement is filled with bodies, but you're freaking me out. Let's find an exit." I pointed and made a right turn around a corner. At the end of another hallway was a peeling old door. "Maybe there?"

I jogged up to the door and gave it a little push. It opened with minimal resistance, and I stumbled into the startlingly bright outdoors.

Teeny held up her hands to block the light. "Whew. That sun is brutal." She put on her red cateye sunglasses. "That's better."

Miss May was the last of us to spill out through the door. "Thank goodness we're out. Now we just have to find a way back in."

"Back in?!" Teeny exclaimed.

I shuddered. "Right. I almost forgot. Lillian Edwards. Room 408. We need to talk to her. But... I don't want to."

"Yeah, nobody wants to! We just escaped," Teeny said. "How are we going to get back in? That skinny, scary giant is everywhere. I feel his pale, Siberian husky eyes on me everywhere I turn. What kind of lunatic doesn't like pie? I'm telling you, there's something off about that man."

"I'm pretty sure we all think there's something off about him," I agreed. "He feels most at home in a mental hospital, so..."

"I think stumbling out this rear exit may have been a lucky break," said Miss May. She pointed toward the other end of the building. "Look. See that refrigerated truck parked about a hundred meters from here? That's a food truck."

"You're not hungry, are you?" Teeny asked. "No judgment, of course. I'm just feeling a little too terrified to eat right now. Which, I'll admit, is rare for me."

"I'm not hungry, Teeny." Miss May started walking in the direction of the truck. "But I recognize that truck. It delivers to the grocery stores in town and a couple restaurants too. Dairy. Eggs. Produce. Stuff like that."

"I don't understand why that matters," I said.

Miss May shook her head. "Because the truck is making a delivery right now. Which means we're probably close to the kitchen. If we can find the kitchen, I bet we can locate a freight elevator which will bypass the lobby and take us straight to residential quarters."

Teeny turned down the sides of her mouth, impressed. "Cool plan, May. You know, sometimes I forget why you're the boss. Then you say stuff like that and I remember."

"I'm not the boss," said Miss May.

"Yes, you are." Teeny and I spoke in unison. Miss May rolled her eyes and kept walking toward the truck.

Miss May turned back to us with a smile. "I was right. That's the service entrance for the kitchen. Follow me."

Miss May quickened her stride. I jogged to catch up to her. "Hold on. What's our plan when we get in there?"

"I'll make a sales pitch to the kitchen manager. I'll tell them that we're here to wholesale pies. I've done wholesale pitches before, it will be easy for me. While I distract them the two of you find the freight elevator and sneak upstairs."

"I don't want to go up there without you," I said. "You're usually in charge of the questions."

Miss May sighed. "OK. Find the elevator and flag me down. I'll jump in and we'll all go together. Alright?"

I nodded. In truth, I didn't love the plan. It was loose. There was too much opportunity for something to go wrong. But I didn't have any better ideas so I had no choice but to follow along.

We squeezed past the delivery truck and into a large, industrial kitchen. The place, unlike most of *Five Pines*, was alive with hustle, bustle, and energy. A row of line cooks prepared hundreds of pounds of food. Orderlies rushed in and out, grabbing trays and shucking them onto carts. An angry-looking, square-headed woman presided over everything.

"That must be the kitchen manager." Miss May nodded toward the square-headed woman. "I'll go over and—"

"What are you doing in my kitchen? Who are you?" The square-headed woman spotted us and charged toward us in short, angry steps. "You need to leave."

"Hi! You must be the kitchen manager. I'll be out of your hair before you know it. But first, I'd love to introduce myself to you. My name is Mabel Thomas and I'm here to sell you the most delicious pies you've ever tasted. I can offer a bulk discount and—"

"I don't want pie. I'm happy with my dessert suppliers. Not very delicious but good enough." *Did everyone in this place hate pie?*

"Now there is my issue. Good enough is never good enough in my book."

The square-headed woman and Miss May argued back and forth about the importance of quality dessert. Meanwhile, Teeny and I edged away from the confrontation and further into the kitchen.

Miss May pulled out a pie and "accidentally" dropped it

on the floor to distract the woman. And with that, Teeny and I made our break and rushed toward the back of the room.

We spotted an orderly pushing a cart of a food card into an enormous, steel elevator. My eyes widened. "Must be the freight elevator. Miss May was right."

"Let's wait a minute. Once the orderly is gone, we'll signal May and head up to the fourth floor." Teeny rubbed her hands together. "We're good at this, aren't we?"

I chuckled. "We're no *Jenna and Mr. Flowers*, but we're OK."

"No one is as good as *Jenna and Mr. Flowers*, Chelsea. No one."

Thirty seconds later, Teeny and I were frantically attempting to catch Miss May's eye — without attracting anyone else's attention. But it was no use. Miss May was in a very heated debate with the square-headed woman. I knew Teeny and I would have to proceed alone.

Thirty seconds later, Teeny and I scurried into the freight elevator. I jammed the button for the fourth floor and the lift lurched into motion. Thirty seconds after that, the door opened and we stepped out into a residential hallway with no receptionist there to stop us in our tracks.

Teeny turned to me with an unsure look in her eyes. "What now?"

"Now we try to find room 408. And try to see if Lillian Edwards killed her roommate."

We walked down the hall, counting off the numbers until we got to room 408. The door was ajar, so I slowly pushed it further open.

Teeny and I lurched into the room, expecting to find Lillian. But instead, all we found was a clean, tidy space made up for the next patient. A tucked-in bed, a guest chair, a simple desk... No killer or potential killers in sight.

"Lillian's gone," I said, as I stepped deeper into the room.

"Maybe she's just on a walk." Teeny followed me inside.

"I don't think so." I pointed around the room as I talked. "Closet's empty. The thermostat is off.

And there's not a single personal effect in the whole place."

"Strange," Teeny said. "Maybe she escaped out the window?"

I scratched my head. "Maybe. I doubt it, though." I crossed the room and looked out the window. "Unless she can fly."

From up on the fourth floor, there was a nice view of the pine trees, stretching in a seemingly endless line toward the horizon. Teeny stood beside me. "I love August. Not just because it's my birthday month. I like how green everything is, how it smells like summer and fall at the same time."

"I'm sure it smells better out there than it does in here. This place is so antiseptic."

"Antiseptic? What does antiseptic smell like?"

I chuckled. "Like...cleaning fluid and doctors."

"Why not just say that?"

I shrugged. "I dunno. Even though I'm enjoying this nice view, I think we should probably head—"

"Can I help you?" A male doctor, in his 50's, stood in the doorway. His eyebrow was raised in suspicion.

"Yes. You can help us." Teeny offered the doctor a nervous smile. "I... You can help us... With..."

"It's OK. You don't need to say anything else. Come on with me and I can help the two of you find your way back to your rooms." The doctor stepped aside and gestured for us to step out into the hall.

Teeny's jaw dropped. "Oh, we're not patients here. We're visitors. Our minds are perfectly healthy. At least for the time being. I think. I mean, we're strange but we don't need to be institutionalized. Not yet."

"Not headed toward a future of being institutionalized, either," I said. "Fingers crossed."

Teeny nodded. "Right."

I stepped forward and tried to speak in a calm and measured voice. It came out high and squeaky. "The tall, pale gentleman let us in to visit our friend."

"The one with the uh, striking, blue eyes," said Teeny.

The doctor furrowed his brow. "Oh. Alright. You should have said that. But who are you visiting? This room is empty."

I tried to smile, but it came out more like a grimace. "It is empty, yes. That's part of our confusion. Our friend Lillian Edwards is supposed to be in this room. Did you know Lillian?"

"Of course. If I recall correctly..." The doctor pulled a tablet out of his bag and opened up a file. "That's what I thought. Lillian was permitted temporary recess from the institution and she never returned."

Teeny's head snapped back in shock. "So she's just out there in the wild? All by herself? No one is watching her or anything?"

The doctor shrugged. "I suppose not. Patient intake and recess are not my department."

"Well how do you know she's OK?" Teeny asked.

"I don't."

"Do you know... when she, uh, checked out?" I inquired.

The doctor flicked through to another screen on a tablet, then stopped. "It looks like Lillian checked out last Thursday."

"Like...two days before Saturday, Thursday?" I asked with my weird squeaky voice.

The doctor nodded. “Yes that is how the days of the week work. You two can show yourselves out. You know the way out?”

I gave the doctor a small nod but I was too shocked to speak. He left, continuing down the long hallway, and Teeny turned to me. “Chelsea. Are you OK? What’s going on?”

“The doctor said Lillian left the hospital last Thursday, right?”

Teeny nodded. “Yeah. So what?”

I looked Teeny in the eyes. “So that means she was out before Beth died. Not just in time to give the eulogy...but also in time for the murder.”

“So you think that’s proof...”

I gulped. “I don’t know if it’s proof. But I think we need to find Lillian Edwards. Fast.”

29

CHECKED OUT

Teeny and I hurried back to the freight elevator and rode back down to the kitchen. I think we were both pretty scared because neither of us said anything. No matter how many times you confront a murderer or get close to learning the truth in a big investigation, those moments never cease to be shocking.

On the one hand, I was glad not to be some sort of jaded, grizzled veteran of murder investigations. That would have been sad. On the other hand, I wished both of my hands would stop shaking and my heartbeat would slow the heck down.

When we emerged out of the freight elevator and into the kitchen, Miss May was still talking to the square-headed woman. Well, the square-headed woman was talking. Miss May was waiting with her most impatient "I'm trying to be patient" face.

Miss May interrupted the square-headed woman's diatribe as we approached. "I understand your point, Matilda. I appreciate that you're running a large-scale operation here. But you can't deny a delicious pie. I can deliver these pies at a five or ten percent lower rate than what I normally do. I'm almost losing money on that deal. This could be a good relationship. I'm only offering you this deal because I feel so strongly that even those of us whom society has marginalized deserve to eat well."

The square-headed lady, whose name I assumed was Matilda, shrugged. "I'm sorry. To be honest I don't like the pie."

Miss May batted her eyelashes. That was the first and last time I ever heard anyone say anything disparaging about Miss May's pie. From the look on Miss May's face, it was a new experience for her too. "What do you mean you don't like the pie?" Miss May laughed. "This pie is award-winning. The apples are picked from my orchard. I'm using a recipe that I've worked on for decades. The crust is often called divine. Once an elderly man took a bite of my pie and it literally killed him with joy. May he rest in peace."

"I don't like it."

I took a ginger step forward. "Excuse me. Sorry. But uh, we're back and we're ready to go."

"Back from where?" The square-headed woman look suspicious.

"The...bathroom," I said. "We found the bathroom. And we both really had to go so it took a while."

Teeny pointed a finger in the air. "Yes. I have irritable bowel syndrome. IBS for short. I'm also just irritable. And I really would like to leave this horrible institution. If you don't like my friend's pie, then you should be upstairs with the patients. Because it is the most delicious, scrumptious, buttery, luscious pie I have ever eaten. I'm proud to call it my favorite pie. Now if you'll excuse us."

Teeny charged away. I followed behind her. Miss May held her chin in the air with pride. "Yes. Please excuse us."

My aunt spun on her heels and followed right behind Teeny and me.

Back in the car, Miss May could not believe what we told her about Lillian Edwards. "You sure you went to the right room?" She turned up the air conditioner and wiped sweat from her brow.

"Yes, May. 408. Not complicated. We talked to the doctor and everything."

"So she's really missing." Miss May sighed. "She could be on the run. But it's also possible she just didn't want to go back to that place. That square-headed kitchen lady was a nightmare. And don't get me started on the skinny guy with the Siberian husky eyes. The whole place sketched me out."

"Good point," I said. "The fact that she didn't return after temporary recess doesn't necessarily mean Lillian killed Beth. It could also mean she just didn't want to go back to that life."

Miss May nodded. "And the fact that Lillian was out in the world before Beth's murder doesn't necessarily mean Lillian killed Beth either. In fact, perhaps Lillian learned of the murder plot somehow and left the institution to warn Beth. They were roommates, after all. And since Lillian gave the eulogy, I presume there was some level of friendship or dedication there."

"I could never be friends with Beth." Teeny took a sharp left turn and headed back toward Pine Grove. "I don't like hanging out with anybody who accuses my friend Chelsea of murder."

I chuckled. "That makes sense. Good criteria for choosing your friends. I don't think I could be friends with Beth either. Because I don't like to hang out with people who accuse me of murder."

"I think it's clear none of the three of us could be friends with Beth," said Miss May. "Moot point, since she's dead. We need to figure out what to do next. Because the poor girl deserves justice, even if we wouldn't hang out with her. And goodness knows the cops aren't going to make anything happen."

"How are we going to find Lillian?" I asked. "That's what we should do, right?"

"Maybe her home address was on those papers in the hospital," Teeny said. "We could go back for them. Or you guys could. Solo mission."

"No point. I photographed the papers with my phone in the record room," I said. "Lillian's home address isn't on there. It's only internal information."

"Let's go talk to Liz at the *Pine Grove Gazette*. She's got the scoop on everyone." Teeny increased the speed of the car by five or ten mph.

Miss May shook her head. "I like the way you're thinking, Teeny. But Lillian wasn't from Pine Grove. If she were local, we'd know her. She must have been from Blue Mountain like Beth. I doubt the editor of our paper will be able to help."

"Let's think of who we know in Blue Mountain," said Teeny.

"I don't need to think about it. I don't know anyone. That place is barely a town," Miss May said. "I've never been there except to deliver food to Beth those few times."

"Yeah I have no Blue Mountain acquaintances," I said.

"Me neither," said Teeny. "I don't want to know those Blue Mountain people. Nothing against them but so far I only know Beth and Lillian and both those girls creeped me out."

I leaned forward and stuck my head between Teeny and Miss May. "Hold on a second. Maybe there was a clue in

Lillian's eulogy. She mentioned a few weird things in that speech, didn't she?"

"Oh yeah." Miss May rubbed her chin. "She talked about laughing at the edge of a rainbow or something."

"Exactly." I scooched further toward the front of the car. "She mentioned a painted lady with gorgeous nails. And a traitor at the end of the bar. What if that wasn't just rambling nonsense? What if those were clues?"

Miss May glanced in the rearview mirror and made eye contact with me. She chuckled. "Chelsea. Sometimes I wonder if your college education was worth anything. Because you can be klutzy and ditzy and very silly a lot of the time."

"But...?" I prompted. "Is there a but at the end of that sentence?"

"But sometimes you're brilliant," Miss May said. "I bet those references in the eulogy are absolutely clues about where Lillian and Beth used to hang out."

"For real?"

Miss May grinned and turned to Teeny. "Teeny. Make your next right. I think I know where we'll find Lillian. But we need to get there fast."

Teeny pressed her foot all the way down on the gas pedal. "Not a problem, May. Not a problem."

30

OVER THE RAINBOW

Fifteen minutes later, we were in the small river town of Peekskill, New York. We had been to Peekskill on prior investigations and every time we drove through the quaint downtown, my heart warmed. Peekskill was a Revolutionary War-era town. It had a mix of old colonial homes, grand Victorians painted in bright colors, and brick factory buildings from the industrial boom in the late 1800's.

Although the small town had gone through some hard times in the 1990's, a recent revitalization effort had transformed Peekskill into a bustling artistic community. That day, an African drummer soulfully beat a djembe in the gazebo, entertaining a small crowd of people. A group of schoolchildren made chalk art on the sidewalk. And a long-haired burnout emerged from a quirky guitar shop with a new guitar slung over each shoulder.

Teeny parked on the main street in town (which was called Division Street, not Main Street), right outside the guitar shop. She hopped out of the car. Miss May and I followed. "What are we doing back in the Skill?" I asked.

I'd asked Miss May the same question several times on the drive over, and she had refused to answer. Nothing changed upon our arrival.

"I told you. You'll know it when you see it." Miss May looked around the little downtown area. "I love this town. Can't you smell the Hudson River on the air?"

Teeny stood on her tippy-toes and sniffed. "I smell French fries and hot wings. And wine."

I laughed. "You can't smell wine."

Teeny turned to me. "Maybe you can't. But I can smell wine from a mile away. Delicious, sweet, wine with two ice cubes."

Teeny's signature beverage was white wine with ice cubes. I have to admit, it was refreshing, although unorthodox. And I thought maybe I'd even get some ice cold wine at dinner that night.

"Can we have dinner in Peekskill?" I asked. "I could go for a wine slushy."

Teeny grinned. "That's my girl."

Miss May headed down the sidewalk toward Main Street (the real one — *confusing, I know*). "As a matter of fact, we're headed someplace with a wonderful selection of dinner fare. I think I'll get a burger with a side of mystery. And maybe they can top it off with a solution to this crime."

"I'll have the same," I said.

Teeny shook her head. "Not me. Not in the mood for a burger. And I don't want anything mysterious on top of my food. If I can't name the ingredient, don't serve it to me. That's what I always say in my restaurant. I hate surprises. Simple food is the answer all the time. Anyone who tells you otherwise is lying straight to your face and they probably hate you."

Miss May and I laughed. "I like that attitude," said Miss

May. "But don't worry. The place we're going is nice and rustic, just how you like it."

Miss May pointed out a small brick building across the street. It had a cute shingle roof and a chimney in the back. "That's the spot. *Revere's Tavern*."

I wrinkled my brow. "Like Paul Revere?"

Miss May nodded. "Yes. This restaurant is rich with Revolutionary War history. In fact, they say this is where Benedict Arnold decided to betray the American troops."

"I'll never forgive that guy." Teeny crossed her arms. "What a Benedict Arnold."

Miss May waited for a few cars to pass then she jogged across the road. Teeny and I strolled behind her, then entered the restaurant.

Did I say restaurant? I meant bar. Bar that served food. *Fine. I suppose tavern is the perfect word for it.*

There was a long wooden bar along the left wall. The opposite side of the room had a few booths. A projector was silently playing *The Wizard of Oz* on one wall. A handmade canoe hung over the shelves of liquor. The whole place had a dark, lively energy.

The place was filled with people drinking, laughing and eating. There had to be a hundred people crammed near the bar. And every table was full. I pointed to a sign that said, "Please Seat Yourself."

"Should we try to grab one of these tables when they open up?"

"Way ahead of you," said Teeny. She darted across the room just as a group of four stood up from a booth. She slid into the booth before the group even had a chance to gather their things from the bench. She smiled. "Sorry. No hurry. Just wanted to make sure we got a seat."

The group of four hurried away, perplexed. Miss May and I joined Teeny in the booth.

"Alright. Now will you finally tell us why we're here?" I asked.

Miss May raised her eyebrows. "You tell me. Look around." I looked around the room, trying to gather clues. First, I scanned the patrons, looking for Lillian. I didn't see her. Then I looked at the walls. There were portraits of the Founding Fathers, but with a modern twist. There was an image of George Washington wearing a silly hat. There was a group of soldiers eating fast food. Then I saw a painting that caught my eye. It was, once again, George Washington. He was at the foot of a rainbow, collecting treasure. He and another man were laughing like they had just heard the funniest joke in their lives. "Laughter at the edge of the rainbow," I said. "Lillian referenced that painting in her eulogy."

Next I spotted a portrait of a woman. She looked practical and reasonable except her fingernails were long and painted bright pink with polkadots. I chuckled. "And there's the painted lady with gorgeous nails."

Miss May touched her nose to indicate that I had gotten the question right. "You're missing one more clue," she said.

I shrugged. "What?"

Miss May pointed at the bar. "The traitor at the end of the bar. Look closely."

I looked back at the bar. It was all smiling, joking faces. Nothing of note particularly. Then I noticed one person at the bar wasn't moving at all. He was, in fact, as still as a statue, dressed in Revolutionary War-era attire. "Is that a statue of Benedict Arnold at the end of the bar?"

"You got it," said Miss May.

"What a creep," said Teeny. "Who wants a statue of that loser in their bar?"

Miss May shrugged. "It's kitschy. More importantly, this is clearly the spot where Beth and Lillian hung out. I've got a feeling Lillian might be here tonight if we wait long enough. And if not, we might find someone to talk to that will have valuable information."

"Good idea. I love it. But first, somebody needs to get us some drinks, Chelsea." Teeny said. She and Miss May looked right at me.

I groaned. "There's like one million people at that bar. I'll never get through to order drinks."

"You will if you try hard enough," said Miss May. "I believe in you."

Teeny grinned. "So do I, Chelsea. You can do anything if you put your mind to it. I'll have a giant glass of white wine with ice in it."

Miss May laughed. "I'll have some kind of British beer. Keep with the theme of the place."

After five minutes of pushing and mumbling "excuse me," I finally made it to the front of the bar. Then began the complicated ritual of trying to catch the bartender's eye long enough to place an order. Every time he looked in my direction I held up my pointer finger and leaned forward. But he looked past me like I wasn't even there. Finally, a gruff woman appeared at the bar next to me and barked toward the bartender. "Hey. Can we get some help over here? Ladies need to drink, too."

I turned to thank the lady, but my gratitude lodged somewhere in the middle of my throat. I was standing at the bar right next to Lillian Edwards, our number one suspect.

I just wanted some icy wine...not a confrontation with a possible killer.

31

REVERE BEER

"This place is so ridiculous. You have to wait forever for them to serve you. It drives me crazy. I just want a drink, you know? To take the edge off. I hate the edge more than anything." Lillian did not seem to recognize me. She slurred her words a bit when she spoke. I assumed she was already pretty tipsy. I would be tipsy too if I were on the run from a mental institution after having killed my former roommate. *Allegedly.*

"Yeah. It's hard to get served at bars sometimes. Especially if you're a woman. So annoying."

"Annoying. Right. That's the perfect word. I'm annoyed by this. That's why whenever I come up here, I get two or three drinks at a time so I won't have to come back. And I'm a regular at this place. This is my spot. They ought to respect me."

I swallowed. "Oh. You come here a lot? I'm just visiting. I run a...milk farm upstate. We make lots of milk and sometimes we deliver down here. It's the best milk in the world."

Note to self: don't make up weird lies about milk when you don't know anything about milk.

"OK. So you're into milk, I guess. No offense, but I'm not really in the mood for milk right now. I want alcohol."

I saw a flicker of sadness in Lillian's eyes and decided to steer the conversation toward Beth. "Alcohol is superior to milk in many ways. I particularly enjoy alcohol when I'm upset or angry or hurt. It's not healthy but sometimes you need to numb the senses, you know? Especially if life has been stressful."

"Right on." Lillian tried to flag down the bartender and failed. "I hate this guy."

I leaned toward Lillian. "Are you feeling stressed? What's going on? We might as well talk it out if we're going to be waiting for these drinks."

"I'm not stressed. Nothing's wrong." Lillian looked away and I saw her chin quiver. She wiped her face on her sleeve then turned back to me. "OK fine. Yeah, I'm feeling some stress. My best friend just died. It was a tragedy. She was killed."

I gasped (a little too loud) to feign shock. "That's terrible. She was murdered? In a small town like this?"

Lillian shook her head. "No. Someone killed her a couple towns over. On a dumpy little apple orchard apparently."

"It's not dumpy." I cleared my throat. "I mean…I like apple orchards. They aren't usually dumpy. I'm not sure which one you're talking about."

"The worst part is I think I know who killed her."

"You do?"

The bartender trundled over to us. He was a big guy with thin-rimmed glasses and a goatee. "Hey, ladies. What will it be?"

"Mikey. I've been here for ten minutes," Lillian said. "This is crazy."

Mikey shrugged. "Busy night. I'm doing my best. I'm alone back here."

"We're all alone in the world," Lillian said. "That's no excuse."

The bartender turned to me. "Do you know what you want?"

Lillian shoved her way between me and the bartender. "Two pitchers of beer please. Something light and cheap. And I want full pitchers not those three-quarter pours like you normally do."

The bartender rolled his eyes and turned to me. "And you?"

"Can I have some kind of British beer, please? And two big glasses of white wine with ice cubes in 'em."

"You want to pay now or do you want to start a tab?"

I handed the bartender cash. "I'll take care of all the drinks. Mine and hers."

The bartender took the money without saying a word and walked away. I expected Lillian to thank me for buying her drinks, and hopefully loosening her lips, but she was too caught up in other things.

"I hate that guy," Lillian said. "The bartender who used to work here was so sweet. She was such an airhead, she forgot to charge me half the time. It was amazing. This guy never forgets. And he doesn't give me any discounts even though he knows my best friend just got killed."

"Oh yeah. You were saying...you think you know who killed her? That's so crazy. Who was it?"

"Why are you asking so many questions?" Lillian glanced around and a paranoid look drifted across her eyes. "Who are you? What do you care?

"I'm just a humble milk lady. I'm nice. I bought your drink." *Uh-oh. My foot was dancing near my mouth again...*

"Oh yeah. What was up with that? Why would you buy my drink? I don't like that."

"You said you had lost a friend. I was just...trying to offer a kindness. That's all. It's nothing to read into. I thought you might like a friendly gesture in your time of need."

Lillian scowled. "Kindness. I don't need kindness. I need my beers. I need to get outta here!"

Lillian's breathing quickened. I suddenly remembered that she was supposed to be living in a mental institution, and that she might be dangerous or unpredictable. I tried to soften my tone. "You're right. I'm sorry. I didn't mean to upset you."

"Stay away from me, milkmaid. Stay away."

Lillian elbowed me aside and started making her way through the crowd, toward the tavern exit. "Hold on. I'm sorry," I called after her.

Lillian picked up her pace and shoved an older man aside. She weaved between patrons with violent determination. I took a few steps to try to catch up, but the gaps Lillian created immediately sealed back up with people.

I watched as she exploded out of the tavern and onto the street. I got out to the street about thirty seconds later, but she had disappeared.

I threw my hands up in exasperation. I had just gotten close to gathering an essential clue in our investigation.

But I had never felt further from the truth.

32

THE ONE THAT GOT AWAY

I turned to reenter the restaurant just as Miss May and Teeny exited onto the street. "Chelsea. What happened in there?" Miss May's brows were knitted with concern.

"Lillian." I shook my head. "She was in there. She was talking to me. I let her get away."

I put my head in my hands. My eyes were pulsing and hot in my head. I had blown my moment to wrap up the investigation. Just because I was bad at telling people to move.

Miss May wrapped her arm around my shoulder. "Hey. You did a good job. It's crazy in that tavern. Don't be upset."

I nodded, although I didn't feel better. "OK. Thank you."

"What did she say?" Teeny asked. "Did she confess? Is Lillian the killer?"

"I don't think she's the killer." I said. I shook my head. "She told me she thinks she knows who murdered Beth. I don't think she would have said that if she was guilty."

"Maybe Lillian recognized you from the funeral?" Miss May suggested. "People are starting to know our faces in

Pine Grove and in surrounding towns. If Lillian knew who you were, she might have given you a bogus story and run away."

"I didn't see any recognition in her eyes. She talked to me for a long time before she freaked out and left. I guess you could be right. But I think she was telling the truth," I said. "At least about her innocence. I don't think she knew me and I don't think she had any reason to lie. I mean, unless she was trying to misdirect us. But I don't know. My gut says Lillian didn't kill Beth."

"Do you think she really knows who the killer is?" Teeny asked.

I looked down Main Street off toward the horizon as though I might still spot Lillian in the distance. She wasn't there. "I'm not sure. She reminded me of Beth in some ways. Paranoid, scared."

"Perhaps delusional?" Miss May's mouth turned down in sympathy. "They were roommates in a mental institution, after all."

I nodded. "I thought that. Lillian is clearly going through a hard time. Maybe she murdered Beth, maybe she didn't. Either way, her roommate is dead. She's a fugitive from *Five Pines*. I think she's been drinking a lot."

"So we're at a crossroads," said Miss May. "If we think Lillian is a reputable source the wisest decision would be to try and find her. She claims she has information on the killer and if that's true, it's the best lead we have."

"But if we don't think Lillian is a reputable source..." I sighed. "There might be better avenues for us to pursue at this moment."

Miss May nodded. "That's right. Especially, of course, if you truly believe Lillian is innocent."

I held up my hands. "I mean, I can't know for sure. You

can never know anything for sure in these investigations. But the way she was talking...I don't know. She was all over the place. I think we should keep her on the list of suspects but we don't need to hurry to find her right now. I'm not sure what that would entail and I think we might be able to spend our time more wisely."

Teeny pouted. "That's too bad. I'm in the mood for a big, wild chase. *Jenna and Mr. Flowers*-style...on horseback, galloping through the grassy knolls, on the heels of the killer."

"That will come later," said Miss May. "But we need to be rational right now. If we make a big scene or start looking around for Lillian, that might scare her anyway. We don't want her to leave Peekskill. We want her to stay where she is in case we need to talk to her later."

"So what do we do now?" Teeny asked.

"Well, what other clues do we have? We know the brothers were financially strapped... I'm not exactly sure how that's motive, but Beth had debt and money makes people do crazy things," Miss May said.

"Yeah, but I think we need to give them a pretty wide berth right now..." I said. "I mean, since Jonathan almost shot at us and I had to spend three-quarters of a night in jail."

"So what do you think we should do?" Miss May asked.

"I think we should go back to those tarot cards," I said. "I'm convinced there was a message in those cards, the way they were laid out in front of Beth. If we can translate that message I think it might help us crack this case."

"Maybe we should get a book and learn about our cards. Or look it up online," said Miss May.

I shook my head. "I had a friend in college who loved this kind of psychic stuff. She always insisted that there was such grace and nuance to the art of tarot. She complained that people think they can read about it in books and 'learn the craft,' and they misinterpret what they see all the time."

"So we need to find a real tarot card reader." Miss May ran her lips across her teeth. "I don't know any other than Salazar and he doesn't want to help us."

"I agree," I said with a sigh. "Salazar or Big Jim are the only people who might be able to read the spread in town. We shouldn't go to either of them anyway. One of them might be involved in all this. I don't think we can trust a potential suspect to give us an accurate interpretation of the cards if what the spread meant was, 'Hey Beth I'm going to kill you and my name is Jim.'"

"That's a bit literal," Miss May said.

"Yeah, I don't know tarot," I said. "And I was exaggerating for effect."

Teeny cleared her throat. "I have an idea."

Miss May and I both turned to look at Teeny. "Go on," I said.

"We can go to this celebrity tarot card reader I heard about," she said.

"How did you hear about a celebrity tarot card reader?" I asked.

Teeny pointed to a flier in the window of *Revere's Tavern*. It was an ad for a celebrity tarot card reader in New York City. "Local advertising."

Miss May laughed. "Good eye, T."

"Do you think we can get an appointment with a famous tarot reader?" I asked.

Teeny shrugged. "Who needs appointments. She probably already knows we're on our way to see her."

33

NOT IN THE CARDS

We piled out of Teeny's convertible and onto the sidewalk in New York City's Greenwich Village.

Back when I had lived in the city with my ex-fiancé Mike, the Village had been one of my favorite places for a Friday night walk in summer. Even though I'd often been in the middle of an argument with Mike, I still thought there was an undeniable romanticism about the cobblestone streets, charming townhouses, and tree-lined sidewalks of the Village.

The good memories outweighed the bad. And that night, when I took a deep breath of the summer air in the city, I exhaled with a smile. "I love it here."

Miss May and Teeny both wore the same placid smiles on their faces. "Me too," said Miss May. "I remember back when I was a prosecutor for the city, we'd come to the Village for drinks after a tough case. Sometimes stay out till two or three in the morning."

Teeny giggled. "Only two or three? When I was running

around with those magicians in my 20's we would stay out till five or six. And that's before the after-hours clubs."

I laughed. "You two were crazy."

Miss May shook her head. "We were crazy. We were young."

"Same thing," said Teeny. "Anyway, I'm still young. I've just changed my office hours."

"We're lucky we got a parking spot so close to the tarot card reader," I said. "My phone says we should be right on top of it. But do either of you see the storefront?"

Miss May muttered as she looked around. "Elaine the psychic, Elaine the psychic, Elaine the psychic..."

Teeny jumped a foot in the air and pointed. "I found it. See?"

I followed Teeny's finger across the street. She was pointing at an elegant restaurant called *Dirt and Salt.*

"That's a restaurant," I said.

"In the basement." Teeny turned to me with a grin. "Down the little stairs. You can see the neon sign and the symbol of a palm opening up."

I stepped into the street and squinted. Sure enough, I could spot the glowing neon lights from the basement beneath *Dirt and Salt*. The neon cast a warm, inviting glow across the cement steps. I took another step toward the shop. A yellow cab sped past me, honking its horn.

"Be careful, Chelsea."

I looked back at Miss May and Teeny with wide eyes. "All this time living in Pine Grove, I've forgotten how to walk in New York City. Gotta look both ways."

Miss May linked one of her arms in mine and the other in Teeny's. "Come on. I'll lead the way."

Quiet wind chimes sounded as we stepped into Elaine's psychic reading parlor. The room was small, but distinct.

There was a psychedelic, paisley purple rug. The walls were white with floral tapestries dangling from the ceiling. There was a small table in the center of the room. Elaine rose from behind the table as we entered.

Elaine the psychic was a beautiful woman. Somewhere in her 50's, she looked Middle Eastern, Persian maybe. She had bright, white teeth and caramel-colored skin. I was jealous of her dark eyebrows and piercing, hazelnut eyes. "Welcome. I'm Elaine. You don't have an appointment."

"No," I said. "We don't."

"I knew from the way you entered. Like you are hoping for me to make an exception to my 'by appointment only' rule. OK. I will, but only this once, and only because you seem desperate. I perform psychic readings, palm readings, and, of course, tarot card readings. I typically read one person at a time however the three of you can remain in the room if that's what you prefer. Who would like to go first?"

I stammered, unsure how to respond to Elaine's wordy greeting. Miss May stepped forward with a nod and held out her hand to shake Elaine's. "Good to meet you, Elaine. As it happens, we're here for a bit of an unorthodox reason."

Elaine smiled. "Most people who come to me are here for unorthodox reasons. Tell me more. Please, sit." Elaine took a seat in the chair behind the desk. Miss May, Teeny, and I sat across from her.

"We discovered a tarot card spread in the bakeshop we own." Miss May looked over at me and Teeny.

I nodded and continued, "Our bakery was closed but someone broke in and laid out these tarot cards. We think it might've been a message to us but we're not sure. We don't know how to read tarot cards and we heard you're the best."

I thought it best not to mention Beth or the murder. Miss May and Teeny seemed to implicitly agree.

Elaine pursed her lips. "Interesting. So you think this spread of tarot cards might've been a message."

Teeny leaned forward. "Or a warning. We've solved a lot of—"

I nudged Teeny and cut her off. "We've solved a lot of puzzles. Miss May is a puzzle champion in the tri-state region. So she has a lot of people who want to bring her down. Jealousy, you know."

Teeny nodded. "Right. She's a puzzle champion. I used to call her Jigsaw Jane because of how good she is with jigsaw puzzles. Yep. This one's got endless patience and keen powers of observation. That's what makes her the best in her field. The governor of New York even gave her a commendation for her puzzle skills a few years back."

"Interesting." Elaine scanned our faces with a disbelieving smirk. "May I see the photo of the spread?"

Miss May opened the picture on her phone and handed it to Elaine. Elaine turned the phone sideways to get a good view. She pinched and zoomed, inspecting each card carefully. "This is a beautiful deck of cards. I believe they call this the Eternal Deck. I haven't seen many of these lately. Very hard to find."

Neither Miss May, nor Teeny, nor I spoke. A heavy energy hung in the air. None of us wanted to say anything. Even if it was silly, it felt like speaking would jinx the moment or interrupt Elaine's focus.

Elaine spent a few more minutes zooming in on each card. Every few seconds Elaine made a small sound of approval or disapproval or concern. Once she bit her lip and scratched her chin like she was solving a puzzle of her own.

After about a few minutes, she looked up and exhaled deeply. "OK. I believe I understand. I'm surprised this spread was left in your bakeshop. Tarot card readings require the energy of the recipient to be present in the room. The recipient must set their intentions before the reading in order to receive an accurate message. Although I suppose it's not impossible that whoever left these cards relied on an intuition or sixth sense for their perception. Although it's also possible they laid out the cards for themselves and not for one of you."

Miss May looked over at me. "We hadn't thought of that."

Teeny bit her fingernails. "What does it say?"

"It's difficult without understanding the intentions and the question that was being asked specifically. But this much is clear to me... This spread indicates that the person receiving the reading had a horrible childhood. There was trauma there. There were difficulties to overcome. These cards indicate that hope is vital. It always is. But this last card, this is what concerns me. See the skeletal knight riding the white horse?" Elaine extended the phone toward us, zoomed in on a particularly sinister card.

Indeed, there was the tarot card she described. She took a deep breath, then spoke as if she was plunging into cold water. "That is the card for death. It is subject to a variety of interpretations. But in this context... It seems to indicate that the recipient's death may be imminent."

Teeny gasped and stood up in a flurry. "So the murderer gave Beth this reading before he killed her. He wanted to scare her. He wanted to add drama to the killing! The killers always add drama in my shows. That's so unnecessary. Like a cat with a mouse! Just kill the poor thing already, you sick cat."

Elaine stood too. "You found this spread at the scene of a murder? You lied to me."

Miss May held up her hands apology. "I'm sorry. We didn't... We shouldn't have..."

"I can't have this energy in my studio. I knew there was something off about your entrance. Please go immediately."

Miss May, Teeny, and I stood and hurried out of the studio. I looked back at Elaine just before we exited.

She looked scared. And her fear really scared me.

34

PIZZA IS THE BEST MEDICINE

We stumbled out onto the street and I said the first words that popped into my head: "I need pizza."

Miss May hung her head and chuckled. "That's what you're thinking about right now?"

"That's what I'm thinking about too, honestly," said Teeny. "When I'm scared I need pizza. It's a fact of life."

We began walking down the street in no particular direction, as New Yorkers often do.

"That was pretty freaky," said Miss May. "I feel bad. We shouldn't have misled her."

"Sorry I blew our cover," Teeny said. "I just couldn't believe it."

Miss May ran her tongue across her cheek. "It's alright. We should all know by now, it's never a good idea to lie to a psychic."

"Yeah, plus, none of us are very good liars. At least, Teeny and I aren't," I said.

Teeny clucked her tongue. "You think that woman really

knows the future? Or the past? Do you think she can talk to dead pets?"

Miss May threw up her hands. "I don't know. But why risk it? She seemed like a true authority on tarot cards."

"True," I said. "But do you need to have psychic abilities to read tarot cards?"

Miss May shrugged. "Not sure it matters. Whoever left those cards out clearly was trying to send a message.. The murderer knew tarot. And they knew Beth. They wanted the killing to feel personal and they tailored everything they did to terrify Beth."

"Pizza," I said.

"You mentioned," said Miss May.

"No. Pizza." I pointed down the street. We were half a block away from the most legendary pizzeria in New York City (at least in my book), *John's Famous Pizza*. "That's *John's*, right?" We'd stopped at *John's* during a previous investigation and I was eager for a repeat. I'd take any excuse to get delicious New York City pizza.

Teeny rubbed her hands together. "I'm getting white pizza and breadsticks. And an Italian ice."

It was a little late so we got a table at *John's* without having to wait. We were seated in the booth by the front window. *John's* was small but oozed with undeniable charm.

Both sides of the room were lined with booths. Every booth had been scratched to oblivion by decades of diners scrawling their names and other messages into the wood with their keys. In the far corner of the room there was an old, woodfire pizza oven. A little Italian man tossed dough up in the air, spread big circles of tomato sauce on crusts, and sprinkled cheese with the elegance and poise of a ballerina.

"I love it in here." I smiled. "I knew pizza would make me feel better. And I'm not even eating it yet."

An annoyed Italian-American woman approached with a notepad. "What do you want?"

"We're here for pizza," said Teeny. "It all smells so good. I feel like I want it all."

"So you're not ready to order. Do you want me to come back?"

"No," I said. "We're ready. We'll take a plain pie and a white pie. And three Italian ices, please."

The waitress walked away without saying anything. Miss May shrugged. "I think she likes us."

Ten minutes later, and we were each onto our second slice of pizza. As often happened when we were eating, none us had said much other than some variation of "yum." I'm sure were all deep in thought about the case. And even deeper in thought about our love of pizza. Then something occurred to me about what Elaine had said back at the studio.

"Hold on a second. I think Elaine may have given us an important clue back there."

Teeny and Miss May looked up from their pizza.

"Are you going to tell us or make us suffer?" Miss May took a big bite of a plain slice.

"You always challenge me to observe the clues that you've already noticed," I said. "Now I issue the same challenge to you."

Teeny slumped her shoulders. "I hate this game. I just want to eat my pizza."

I grabbed a slice and smirked. It felt good to finally be the one withholding information.

Miss May put her slice of pizza down. "We can do this, Teeny. Let's think."

Teeny crossed her arms. "Thinking is boring when the alternative is pizza."

"Elaine mentioned that it's possible to give yourself a tarot card reading," Miss May said. "Do you think Beth might have… hurt herself?"

I shook my head. "No. I think she was murdered. That's not the clue."

"Elaine also mentioned Beth's childhood. Maybe the killer was someone Beth knew when she was a kid," Teeny said. "I still have plenty of enemies from my schoolyard days."

"That's an interesting observation. This might have something to do with Beth's past," I said. "But that's not the clue of which I'm speaking."

Miss May's jaw dropped. "I know. I know what it is."

I spread my palms across the table. "Go on."

"The first thing Elaine said when she began the tarot card reading was that the deck was interesting and unique. She implied it was a rare deck."

I smiled. "That's right."

"So what?" Teeny asked.

"Elaine didn't just say the deck was rare," I said. "She gave us the name."

Teeny nodded. "Oh yeah. It was an Eternal Deck. She said it's hard to find."

I touched my nose, like Miss May always did when we were onto something. "That means there aren't a lot of shops that sell the Eternal Deck. If we can figure out which stores stock that particular deck, we might be able to trace the purchase back to the person who bought the deck. It sounds like this Eternal Deck isn't mass-produced. We might have to sort through a lot of sales data from magic stores, but I think this might be a breakthrough."

Miss May chuckled. "We don't have to go through any sales data," she said.

I puffed up my lower lip. "We don't?"

Miss May shook her head. "We just need to find out if Big Jim sells that deck."

35

OUT OF AFRICA

By the time we got back to Pine Grove that night, Big Jim's magic shop was closed. We all agreed we would head over there first thing in the morning. My keys were still missing, so we were planning to continue sleeping at Teeny's... but first, Miss May and I stopped by the farm for a few hours to check up on KP and the animals.

I chatted with See-Saw the tiny horse about the case. She wasn't in the mood to talk. I played fetch with Steve the dog, but he got tired and fell asleep. I petted Kitty, but she just wanted food and lost interest in social interaction as soon as I gave her some tuna. Then, Miss May and I locked up and headed back to Teeny's place for the night.

But when I climbed into bed around 11 PM, I felt lonely. Maybe part of it was sleeping at Teeny's house instead of in my own room, but I knew there was more to it.

The truth was, even though my aunt and Teeny and the farm animals were good company, they weren't the company I wanted. I missed Germany.

Since he had returned to his research in Africa, he and I hadn't been able to connect much. He rarely had Internet access. Besides, he spent most of the time in the field, studying lions. He was so deeply immersed in his work, so cloud-headed, that sometimes he didn't even remember to text when he did have a WiFi connection.

I pulled my covers up to my chin and turned on my side. "I miss Germany," I said out loud. As if by magic, my phone rang. It was a video call. And it was from Germany.

I sat straight up in bed, turned on the light, fluffed my hair, accidentally over-fluffed my hair, de-fluffed my hair, then answered the call. There was Germany, wearing a tan safari hat and smiling from ear to ear. "Chelsea. You look lovely. More radiant than the most radiant lioness on the plains of Africa, and let me tell you, that lioness is radiant. Yet compared to you, all of the wildlife in the jungle is nothing but pebbles on the dirty ground. How are you?"

I laughed for a minute straight. Germany may have traded his rural American denim for African khaki but he had not lost his bizarre way with words. "Hi, Germany. I miss you. I was just thinking about you."

"I'm always thinking about you. This afternoon I found myself passing an Internet café in a small town. That is where I am now. I'm not often here. But I wish I could communicate with you more frequently via phone, video, or telepathic means."

Over the next ten minutes, Germany and I chatted about everything that had been going on since he had left. I tried not to talk too much about the case because I didn't want to bring the conversation down. I wanted to hear about Africa and Germany's work. He was helping research the behavior of a pride of lions in an area where there was a drought. That was as much as I could gather. Although he said a lot of scientific and environmental jargon that sounded very impressive.

Eventually, the connection started to flicker and corrupt. Germany's image pixelated, then disappeared, then reappeared in strange pieces. "Germany. The connection is bad."

His voice replied in choppy half-words, fragmented by the slow Internet. "I... You... Love... Radiant... Miss... Splendid and... Every single day."

"I love you, too," I said. "Good night, Germany."

With that, the screen went black. And I finally managed to fall asleep.

36

THE EARLYBIRD GETS THE MUFFIN

I woke up to the smell of chocolate chip muffins in the air. My nose dragged me out of bed, pulled me into the hallway, and sat me down at Teeny's kitchen table. Miss May had fully made herself at home in Teeny's kitchen. As I entered the room, Miss May pulled a tray of muffins out of the oven and turned to me with a smile. "Morning, Chelsea."

I squinted and looked at the time in the microwave. "It really is morning. 7 AM?"

Miss May shrugged. "I didn't force you out of bed." She placed them up on a plate and put it down in front of me.

"You know muffins wake me up," I said. "So you basically did force me. Why?"

"We've got a big day ahead of us," Miss May said. She sat at the table across from me and broke off the top of one of the muffins.

"I know. But Big Jim isn't going to be open until at least nine or ten. Do you need help with something back on the orchard or in the bakeshop?"

Miss May nodded. "We've been falling behind on our

peach pie orders with this investigation. I was thinking, maybe... We could bake a few pies before going over to Big Jim's?"

I laughed. "How far behind?"

"Twenty pies?" Miss May said with a shrug. "None of them are technically late yet but they will be."

I spread a slab of country butter on the muffin and watched it melt. "Doesn't sound like there's much of a choice."

Miss May took another big bite of muffin. "Smart girl."

A couple minutes later, we'd piled into the VW bus and were rumbling toward the farm.

KP was drinking coffee and grumbling about the morning when we arrived. We said hello, he grouched out a greeting in return, and then we headed straight for the bakeshop.

Do you want to know the secret to perfect peach pie?

The secret is using farm fresh peaches straight from the trees on your family orchard, juicy and delicious and the best in the world. *Alright, maybe that's not helpful advice for the home cook.* But store-bought peaches can be good too. And the real secret is just to use tons of butter in the crust.

Miss May and I worked hard for about three hours. I prepped the peaches and she prepped the dough. I hadn't yet graduated to making the crust. It was an art. But trust me, I saw all the butter she used.

When everything was all set for baking Miss May dusted her hands off on her apron then hung the apron over a chair. "OK. We're almost ready to talk to Big Jim."

I checked the clock. "It's 11 AM. He's open by now. Why aren't we completely ready?"

The oven dinged. Miss May pulled a fresh peach pie out and smiled. "Now we're ready."

Ten minutes later, Miss May, Teeny, and I entered Big Jim's magic shop. Miss May was holding the fresh pie out in front of her. Big Jim narrowed his eyes when he saw her. "No, no, no, Miss May. I'm not going to be questioned like a murderer in my shop. Not again. Leave the pie and get out."

Miss May smirked. "If I go, the pie goes with me. And we're not here to treat you like a suspect." Miss May placed the pie down in front of Jim.

He took a big smell of it and his eyes rolled back in his head. "I bet that's what you tell all the boys." Big Jim winked at Teeny. "How's it going, Teeny? Are you doing something new with your hair? Looks great."

Teeny shook her head. "Nothing new. It's been the same for the past ten years. But thanks for noticing. Now are you going to answer our questions or not?"

"It looks like you're doing something new with it. Very nice."

"Big Dan likes her hair, too," said Miss May. "Remember, he got you that gift certificate for the fancy hair place?"

Teeny smiled. "Yeah. He's the best. Mechanics are my type of man. Practical and level-headed. Good with their hands. Don't have their heads up in the clouds. Not like magicians."

"I'm not a magician," said Big Jim. "I'm a businessman. And last time I brought my car to Big Dan, it came back with a whole new problem."

"I don't believe you," I said. "Big Dan is a handy and reliable mechanic."

Miss May stepped forward to defuse the tension. "Let's calm down, everybody. Jim, you have an amazing fresh pic in front of you. You can eat it all right now if you want. We're not here because we think you're a suspect. We respect that you're a businessman and we're here with business questions."

"Are your business questions related to the murder?"

Miss May shrugged. "We're not sure. But can you show us the tarot decks you sell in this store?"

Big Jim guffawed. "Sure, I guess. My product is top of the line. Even the tarot cards. Beautiful, well-made. You buy a deck from me, you'll never have to buy a deck again."

Big Jim laid three decks of tarot cards out in front of us. The first two were nondescript. But, sure enough, the last deck was labeled, "The Eternal Deck."

Miss May picked up the Eternal Deck. "These ones seem nice. Are they popular?"

"To be honest, none of them are popular. I don't sell a lot of tarot cards. My best-selling products are all magic-based. Magic kits, magic hats, magic meatballs... You get it."

"That makes sense." I took the deck from Miss May. "These are beautiful, though. I would buy them if I was into that sort of thing."

Jim walked back behind the counter, next to his stool. "If you ask me, I still think Sudeer murdered Beth. I guess you have evidence or whatever. But that guy gives me the creeps. He wanted Beth to leave him alone so he took drastic measures. That's my theory."

Miss May nodded. "And we appreciate your input. Any information helps. Solving murders is all about gathering information and making decisions."

"So you need to know what kind of tarot cards I sell in my store? That's vital information to this investigation?"

Miss May tilted her head from side to side. "We don't know if it's vital. We won't know for a while, I don't think. We just want to get the murderer off the streets as soon as possible."

Jim sat on the stool. He groaned as he lowered his body. "We all do. Pine Grove is incredible in so many ways. These murders bring me down."

Teeny looked down. "No, the murders aren't a lot of fun."

"I love my town. And I want to keep it safe," Big Jim said. "So even if I'm wrong about Sudeer...if these tarot cards help you in any way, I'd be glad to have been of service. If you need anything else..."

"As a matter of fact, I think we could use a little more help from you," said Miss May. "You've got a successful business here and you've been around a while. So I'm sure you have a great record-keeping system."

Big Jim nodded. "That's right. My point-of-sale system is top notch."

"Amazing." Miss May looked at me. "We need to work on a better point-of-sale system up at the orchard. We've been using the old family cash register for years."

"It would be good to get all that digitized," I said.

"It's amazing," said Jim. "I can email my receipts to the customers. I can send them promotions. It helps a lot."

Miss May leaned on Big Jim's counter. "Do you think you could look up this Eternal Deck for me? I would love to know if anyone has purchased these cards in the past couple weeks or even in the past month."

"If it will help catch the killer, I'd be happy to." Big Jim entered a search on his computer and scanned the results. "Like I said, I don't sell a lot of tarot cards. I've only sold this pack once in the past six months."

Miss May nodded. "Who bought it?"

Big Jim looked up and made eye contact with Miss May. "Lillian Edwards."

37

ETERNAL QUESTIONS

We stumbled out of Big Jim's magic shop, dumbfounded. Lillian Edwards had purchased the Eternal Deck from Jim. That meant she was our best suspect in the murder. So we needed to find her, fast.

The August sun was scorching hot that morning. The glaring heat was a reminder of the mounting tension in our investigation. It never felt good to have a killer roaming around in your general vicinity. It felt even worse on the hottest day of the year.

I wiped the sweat off my forehead and turned to Teeny and Miss May. "So we need to find Lillian Edwards. Should we go back to the bar?"

Miss May squinted against the sun. "We could try the bar. But I don't think that's going to work. If Lillian is the killer there's no way she's going to go back there. Not after running into you, Chelsea. Especially not after her paranoid behavior."

"I guess you're right," I said. "She's probably in hiding somewhere if she's actually guilty of this murder."

"Something doesn't add up, though," said Teeny. "I thought Lillian was all upset in the bar because she claimed to know who had killed Beth. Why would she have talked that way if she were the killer?"

"Let's not forget she was on a temporary reprieve from the mental institution." Miss May put on her sunglasses. "I support mental healthcare, of course, and I'm not trying to judge anyone for their struggles...but I also know that mental illness can disrupt a person's perception of reality. So, I'd take anything Lillian said with a grain of salt."

I nodded. "That's a good point. It's possible she was talking about herself when she referenced the killer. Maybe she was in the middle of some kind of confession, like...her guilt was compelling her to talk about the murder she had committed in an indirect way."

"OK. It seems to me we need to find her house." Teeny pulled a bottle of water from her purse and took a big sip. "Can we blast the air conditioning in the car during our search? It's got to be 100° out here."

"It's in the 90's for sure," I said. "I didn't realize it was going to be such a scorcher. Murder investigations distract me from the weather. But this is in-your-face heat."

Miss May chuckled. "Murder investigations are distracting. That's why I'm happy we got those peach pies done this morning."

"Still getting good orders?" Teeny asked.

Miss May shrugged. "Yeah, which is great, considering there's been another murder in town. I suppose people like to have their summer comfort foods when they're feeling anxious or stressed."

"Are you totally overwhelmed?" Teeny winced.

"Not totally," said Miss May. "Why are you wincing?"

"I need to order ten pies for the restaurant. People keep asking for your peach pie and I feel bad I ran out."

Miss May laughed. "OK. We'll bake a new batch and get it to you as soon as we can. But it might have to wait until after we find this killer."

Teeny crossed the parking lot and headed toward Miss May's yellow VW bus. "Then let's find this killer fast. People need their peaches! Especially my sister, Peach. She's taken personal offense that she can't get her namesake pie at my restaurant."

Fifteen minutes later and we were cruising through the tiny town of Blue Mountain, New York. We didn't have a plan for how to find Lillian's house and we had no idea where she lived. But Miss May insisted that she could use her small-town charm to get us Lillian's address. My aunt pulled up to a general store, the only store in town, and hopped out. "Alright. I'll be back."

"I'm coming," I said. "Snacks from roadside general stores are the best kind of snacks."

The general store was quaint and surprisingly high-end. There were fancy bags of local sundries. Farm fresh cheeses. Lots of delicious produce.

I grabbed a bag of dried apples. Miss May picked out a granola bar from a local kitchen. And we headed to the counter to check out. The man working the cash register had to be three hundred years old. He was hunched over and he was on a respirator but he lit up with a smile as we approached.

"Welcome to *Blue Mountain General.* Don't recognize the two of you beautiful ladies. I see you picked out some of our finest sundries."

Miss May smiled. "That's right. We drove all the way up here from Virginia to see an old friend. Need to grab some snacks before we surprise her. But you'll never believe what happened..."

"I'm sure I won't," the man rasped.

"I had her address on my smartphone. The phone got us all the way to Blue Mountain. Then I ran out of battery so I lost her address! I don't know what we're going to do. Knock on every door in town?"

"That's one option," said the old man. "You can probably knock on every house within a few hours' time. Not a lot of residents here. Or you could let me know who it is you're looking for and maybe I can help."

"That second option sounds great," said Miss May. "It's hot out there, and going door to door sounds pretty miserable. We're looking for Lillian Edwards."

The man furrowed his brow. "Lillian Edwards? That's Janet's daughter. I'm afraid she hasn't lived in town for almost ten years. She...went away."

"That's right," said Miss May. "I knew she had spent some time... I knew she had some issues... But I heard she had been back in town recently. That's why we came up to see her."

"I haven't heard anything about Lillian being back in town." The old man's eyes hardened. Seems that he didn't appreciate Miss May's allusion to Lillian's hospitalization. Some small-town people loved to gossip. Others thought it was the ultimate sign of disrespect.

"OK." Miss May handed the man a ten dollar bill with a small head nod. "Thank you for your time. Please keep the change."

The man took the money. We left. Although we had delicious snacks in our possession, we were no closer to finding Lillian Edwards or solving the mystery of who killed Beth.

38

SWEATING WEATHER

Miss May and I piled back into the front of the bus to find Teeny with her face smashed against the air-conditioning vent. She slumped over with relief when she saw us. "At last, you're back. I was running out of cold air in here. The air conditioning got 5° hotter every minute you were in there. Turn on the engine. Now. Before I sweat to death. This is real...sweating weather. Like sweater weather but with sweating instead of sweaters. Chelsea, I'm surprised you're not drenched."

"I'm more of a nervous sweater," I said. "But thanks, Teeny."

Miss May turned on the engine with a sigh. Teeny glanced over, concerned. "What's wrong? Small-town charm finally failed you?"

"I think our collective brain failed us, this time." Miss May backed out of the parking lot. "It doesn't make any sense to try to find out where Lillian Edwards lives. She just got out of the mental hospital, remember? She doesn't have a house in town anymore. She might be staying with someone but there's no way she has a permanent address."

"So did you ask the employee in there who Lillian is staying with?" Teeny asked. "That's easy enough."

Miss May shook her head. "Not as easy as it sounds. The elderly gentleman in there isn't much for gossip. He was nice, but I think he thought we were snooping."

"We are snooping." I opened my bag of apple chips and popped one in my mouth.

Teeny leaned forward. "Yum. Apple chips. What'd you get me?"

I froze, my second apple chip suspended inches from my mouth. "Um... We got you a snack. Of course we did. We're always thinking of you."

Teeny nodded. "I know. You two are the best. Kind. Considerate. Thoughtful. So what did you get me?"

I cringed and extended the bag of apple chips toward Teeny. "These apple chips?"

Teeny hung her head. "You forgot me. I'm lucky you came out before I died from heat exhaustion in the car."

I laughed and offered the apple chips to Teeny once again. "Just take a handful."

Teeny took the bag with a smile. "I'll let you know when I'm ready to share."

Miss May, Teeny, and I laughed. Teeny inspected the label on the back. "Hey. This is from McIntosh Farms. May, don't you know the lady who runs the place?"

"I know all the orchard owners in the tri-state area. Mrs. McIntosh is a sweetheart."

"I bet she is." Teeny ate an apple chip. "She makes a great apple chip, too. Why don't you sell apple chips at your orchard?"

"We do," said Miss May.

Teeny responded with a mouthful. "Oh."

"Hold on a second." I looked at Miss May. "You know the owner of a local orchard in Blue Mountain?"

Miss May nodded.

"In my experience owners of community gathering spaces like that have tons of information. I mean, at least that's true for me and you."

Miss May looked over at me. "Go on..."

"So why don't we pay your friend Mrs. McIntosh a visit? She might have up-to-date information about Lillian's whereabouts. At the very least, we can buy a fresh bag of these apple chips since Teeny is going to eat all of mine."

"I like that idea," said Miss May.

Teeny handed the bag of apple chips back to me. There were only a few left. "More apple chips sound good to me."

We rolled up to McIntosh farms just a few minutes later. The place was beautiful. It wasn't more beautiful than the *Thomas Family Fruit and Fir Farm*. Not by a long shot. But it was charming in a different way. The orchard was smaller. And the farmhouse, where Mrs. McIntosh lived, was all the way in the back along the shore of a tiny pond. Ducks floated in the pond and a matronly woman, somewhere in her 60's, tossed out bits of bread for them to eat. Miss May laughed when she saw the woman. "That's Mrs. McIntosh. Always feeding those ducks."

Miss May honked the horn. Mrs. McIntosh looked over and gave us a big wave. She turned away from the pond and met us in the driveway to the farmhouse with her hands on her hips.

"Mabel. What are you doing in Blue Mountain?"

Miss May smiled and hugged Mrs. McIntosh. "Just saying hi."

"You used to come by here once a month, at least. It's been too long. I'm mad at you."

"You are not mad at me."

"I should be." Mrs. McIntosh gestured to me and Teeny. "Who are these beautiful young ladies?"

"This is my best friend, Teeny. And that's Chelsea, my niece."

Mrs. McIntosh smiled at us. "So I've got all three amateur detectives here." She shot a glance over at Miss May. "That's right. I keep up with all the big news in Pine Grove. You three are incredible. Oh no. Don't tell me someone in Blue Mountain died?"

"Not quite," I said. "Sort of..."

Mrs. McIntosh was concerned. "How can someone not quite die? Either you're dead or you're alive."

Miss May chuckled. "You make a good point."

"Stop right there," said Mrs. McIntosh. "We're going to talk. I would love to talk. But you're guests on my orchard. That means you need apples."

Miss May protested. We were there for an investigation. But Mrs. McIntosh wouldn't discuss anything until we joined her in her kitchen for some fresh apple crumble. Well, freshish. It wasn't apple picking season yet, so the crumble was made with apple preserves. Nonetheless, Teeny and I were fine with it. And I secretly think Miss May was, too.

Mrs. McIntosh's kitchen was straight from the pages of *Architectural Digest*. My interior design brain was having a field day as I looked around the charming, elegant space. There was a sunken sink. There were exposed copper pipes. There was a rustic, wooden table right in the center of the room. Honestly, the place reminded me a lot of Miss May's farmhouse. I missed staying there and I hoped we could find the killer soon so we could return home.

"I always forget how wonderful your house is," said Miss

May. "And you've got the time to have apple crumble in the oven?"

Mrs. McIntosh laughed. "I don't do peaches. This is my off-season. I make desserts with apple preserves, and I read books. I've discovered this beautiful hobby called relaxation. You should try it sometime."

Miss May laughed again. "That's good advice. Especially when I've got Chelsea to pick up the slack. What do you think, Chelsea? Can you handle the peach harvest and I'll come up here and hang out with Mrs. McIntosh in the summer months?"

"You won't even let me make the pie dough for the peach pie! You want me to handle the entire harvest?" We all cracked up laughing as we dug into the apple crumble.

Oh... My... Goodness... Apple crumble. Mrs. McIntosh knocked it out of the orchard. The crumbles on top were doughy and crispy and rich with butter and cinnamon. And the layer of apple preserve was like velvet in my mouth. It took every ounce of willpower in my body not to grab entire handfuls from the pan and shove them in my pockets for later.

Once we all tried and praised the apple crumble, Mrs. McIntosh turned the conversation back to the reason for our visit. "Now. Tell me about this person who is not quite dead."

Miss May nodded. "Right. We're here because someone in Blue Mountain has been murdered. And one of your residents is a person of interest in our investigation."

"Do you know Lillian Edwards?" I asked.

Mrs. McIntosh put down her fork and and sighed. "I knew her mother Janet very well. Lillian was a lot like Janet, in many ways. Such a bright light. Sometimes a little too bright. My heart aches for her."

"We saw Lillian speak at the victim's funeral," Miss May said. "She was eloquent. Very interesting."

"Interesting is the perfect word," said Mrs. McIntosh. "You think Lillian is the killer?"

"We're not sure," said Teeny. "We need to talk to her. But apparently the old guy who works at the general store wouldn't provide any information."

Mrs. McIntosh laughed. "You tried to get gossip out of old Isaac? I would have loved to see that. He doesn't make small talk, big talk, or anything in between."

Miss May hung her head. "Yeah our conversation didn't go well. But he did sell us your apple chips."

"Oh good. We sell a lot out of that store. Once the people come up to go apple picking they like their gourmet sundries for the ride home."

"Don't I know it," said Miss May.

"We all do," said Teeny. "I once had some city banker fellow buy every dessert in my dessert case to take back to his friends in Manhattan."

I shrugged. "City people like a little taste of the country life. I was like that once. I'm lucky, now I have it all the time."

Mrs. McIntosh pointed at me. "Smart girl."

Miss May leaned forward. "So have you seen Lillian Edwards around town lately? I know she had been at *Five Pines* for quite a while but she left last week and never returned."

Mrs. McIntosh leaned back in her chair and exhaled. "Oh Lillian is most certainly back in town. And she's not just laying low and freeloading either. She got herself a job."

"So you know where we can find her?" asked Teeny.

Mrs. McIntosh nodded. "Grab a piece of paper. Write this down."

39

DUNKIN' SUSPECTS

Mrs. McIntosh informed us that Lillian Edwards had gotten a temporary job working at a booth at the Blue Mountain summer carnival. Summer carnivals in New York were a special phenomenon, so I was excited to experience one as we tried to find Lillian.

Miss May and Teeny were excited too, and the three of us bubbled over with anticipation as we parked the car near the Blue Mountain fire department and headed toward the big field out back.

The place was packed with happy people from Blue Mountain and presumably from even smaller surrounding towns. A food truck sold curly fries, pizza and funnel cakes. And there were dozens of booths where visitors could throw darts at balloons or toss ping-pong balls into fishbowls or play other carnival games.

"This place is amazing. I feel like I'm ten years old again." I pointed out a little blonde boy who was eating a big bowl of chocolate ice cream. "That was me every summer. Except I had ice cream all over my face and shirt."

Miss May laughed. "You were adorable."

"This is a terrific summer carnival," said Teeny. "We should come every year."

Miss May nodded. "Blue Mountain is nice. Pine Grove is great, so we don't have a ton of reason to leave...but you're right, I would come back for this."

Teeny squinted into the neon lights with her hand on her forehead like a sailor. "Any sign of Lillian?"

Miss May looked at the notes she had written back in Mrs. McIntosh's farm. "Mrs. McIntosh said Lillian is working at a booth all the way in the back of the carnival. Let's pick a direction and walk around until we find her."

"I vote we walk in the direction of the funnel cakes," I said.

Miss May chuckled. "I thought you might say that. Why don't we save the funnel cakes for a reward after we talk to Lillian?"

"If she's the killer, we might get too caught up in the case and forget all about funnel cakes," I said. "I vote we get one now."

Teeny smiled. "I second that vote. The funnel cake will fuel my investigating muscles."

Miss May gasped and covered her mouth. "There she is."

"Where?" I followed Miss May's gaze to a booth about twenty feet away. Indeed, there sat Lillian Edwards, in a dunk tank. She was perched on a bench above a pool of water, challenging people to throw a ball and send her under.

"Hey, mister. You look like you got a strong arm. Grab a softball see if you can dunk me."

"Is that really her?" I took a few steps closer. "Whoa. It is. For some reason I wasn't expecting her to be working the dunk tank..."

Whoosh! The man threw the ball. He hit the target and

Lillian fell into the water with a splash. A small crowd of people clapped and a little boy begged his father for the opportunity to throw the ball next.

Miss May, Teeny, and I drifted over to the edge of the crowd to watch the spectacle and hatch a plan. After a few seconds, Lillian popped out of the water with a smile. "Great shot, mister. Who's next? Who else thinks they can dunk me?" Lillian climbed a small ladder and slid back onto her perch above the water. Just as she got settled, Lillian made eye contact with me. Her eyes widened. I tried to look away but it was too late.

"Five-minute break for me, people. I'll be right back. Need to use the restroom and I don't want to pee in my own dunkin' water."

The small crowd of people laughed as Lillian swung her leg over the side of the tank and descended down an exterior ladder toward the ground.

I edged my way through the crowd, toward the booth. I looked back at Miss May and Teeny. "Let's go. She saw me and now she's trying to get away." *So much for funnel cake.*

By the time we got around to the other side of the dunking booth, Lillian was already a dozen yards away, hurrying toward the edge of the property. She looked back, spotted us and quickened her pace.

"Lillian. Wait." I called after her.

"Stay away from me." Lillian jogged.

"We don't want to hurt you. We're here to help." Miss May tried to jog after Lillian but stopped and held her head after a few seconds. "I can't keep up with her. Chelsea, try to catch her."

"I'm not a runner," I said. "Look at me."

Miss May pointed up at Lillian. "She's getting away. Go."

I took a deep breath and ran as fast as I could after

Lillian. My legs tired in seconds. My chest pounded. My arms flailed for some reason, like I was swatting bugs.

Lillian, on the other hand, appeared to be in great shape. She jumped over a picnic table. She did a spin move around a happy young couple. Then she reached a chain-link fence and jumped onto it, clinging to it like a spider in a web.

"Come on. Wait there, Lillian. You're not going to climb that..."

I was wrong. Lillian climbed the fence with ease, flopped over to the other side, and disappeared, running into the darkness.

I arrived at the chain-link fence, got a toehold and grabbed on. But that was as far as I could go. I tried to climb and slipped back down to the ground. My shirt caught on the fence and ripped. I called once more into the darkness but it was too late. Once again, I'd scared Lillian away.

I hung my head and trudged back toward the carnival. Although I thought I had been running for five minutes straight and that I must have covered at least half a mile, I arrived back at the dunk tank in only one or two minutes.

Miss May and Teeny perked up when they saw me. "Did you talk to her? What did she say?"

I kicked the ground. "I'm sorry. She got away."

Miss May put her hand on my shoulder. "It's OK, Chelsea. I think we had a breakthrough, anyway."

I raised my eyebrows. "Really? How?"

Miss May held up a big, black purse. "Lillian forgot her bag."

40

LOOSENING THE PURSE STRINGS

All three of us piled into the back of Miss May's van. Miss May had long ago converted the rear of the VW bus into a kitchenette for farmer's markets and events. Technically, the kitchenette in the van had been my first interior design job.

Right after my parents died, I'd moved in with Miss May, and she'd wasted no time in offering a cure to my sadness — hard work. I'd worked on the farm, of course, doing menial tasks, but Miss May wanted to offer me more of a challenge. So she'd asked me to design and decorate the little kitchenette.

At first, I'd doubted my ability to undertake such a task. I was a sad, recently orphaned adolescent and I'd never designed anything, let alone a mobile kitchen. But the kitchenette had turned out adorable.

It was a 50s-style design, with a little booth, a colorful, bubbly, retro refrigerator, and a stove where we made hot chocolate. Usually for ourselves, but sometimes for customers.

That day, Teeny and I sat on one side of the booth and

Miss May scooted into the other side. As soon as we were settled, Miss May turned Lillian's purse over and dumped it out on the table. A seemingly endless stream of items poured from the purse. Three different brands of cherry lip balm. Three tattered old Agatha Christie paperbacks. Some duct tape. Two or three handfuls of loose kettle corn.

Finally, something caught my eye...

"That's a book on tarot."

"Where?" Miss May dug through the pile.

"Underneath that popcorn. I can see the cover peeking out. It looks like one of the images from the Eternal Deck." I reached into the pile and removed the palm-sized book with a ginger touch. After I flicked a few sticky popcorn kernels away, the cover of the book was fully visible. "I knew it. Look."

I showed the cover of the book to Teeny and Miss May. It was called "The Essential Guide to Tarot Card Reading," and it was well-worn.

"Good eye, Chelsea." Teeny picked up a piece of the popcorn.

"Don't eat that popcorn," said Miss May.

Teeny clucked her tongue. "I wasn't going to eat loose popcorn from a stolen purse, May. I just wanted to see if it was butter or kettle corn or caramel or what."

"Clearly kettle corn," I said. "I solved that mystery as soon as I felt how sticky the kernels were."

"We'll know for sure if one of us tastes it," said Teeny.

Miss May shook her head. "You are unbelievable."

Teeny laughed. "I'm joking. I'm not going to eat garbage popcorn! I'm not an animal, Chelsea. Now open the tarot book."

I flipped the tarot card book open. The pages were filled with small, dense type. Every so often there was a picture of a tarot card with a long explanation of what it might mean. "It's just like the cover states... A guide to tarot card reading. Not sure how that helps us now."

"Let me see that." Miss May reached out and I handed her the book. She flipped it open and smiled. "This book is far more helpful than you thought, Chelsea."

I shrugged my shoulders. "OK. Great. What did I miss?"

Miss May fanned the book open and showed me the inside cover.

I read aloud, "'If found returned to Lillian Edwards. 6 Hamilton Drive, Blue Mountain, New York.' Whoa." I lurched forward with my eyebrows raised. "She put her address in the book. That's amazing."

Teeny sat back with a grin. "That's good detective work."

Miss May snapped the book closed. "That's luck. Let's head over there soon, before our luck runs out. Strap in, ladies. We're going for a ride."

Miss May climbed from the back of the van up to the driver seat. I caught her by the shoulder. "Hold on. Lillian just left the carnival on foot. That address can't be more than two or three minutes from here by car. If we go there now, she won't even be there yet. We'll beat her home, she'll see us waiting, and we won't be able to ask her anything."

Miss May scooted around to get comfortable and adjusted the rearview mirror. "She doesn't know the car I drive. She won't know it's us. And I want to see her arrive."

Hamilton Drive was nestled in the outskirts of Blue Mountain's dilapidated industrial area. The area was about three blocks long, and it was dotted with abandoned factories and warehouses that had long since gone out of business. There were no people on the streets and there were no lights on in any of the buildings, except for one. You guessed it, the single illuminated building was 6 Hamilton Drive.

Miss May screeched to a halt across the street from the address. There, painted on the brick above a steel door were the words, *The All-Seeing Eye Communal Living Center.*

I squinted to make sure I was reading the words right. "*The All-Seeing Eye Communal Living Center.* That's Lillian's address?"

Miss May cranked the car into park and turned off her headlights. "It makes sense to me. Lillian is a fugitive from *Five Pines.* So she came to this cult for anonymity. These are probably the people who run the carnival. I bet they got her the job in the dunk tank."

"Oh no. I don't do cults. Cults freak me out. I hate drinking the special juice. I do not like the idea of men in long robes. It's all wrong," Teeny said. "We're not going into a cult. That's where I draw the line. Sorry, Beth. The mystery of your murder must go unsolved."

"Quiet down," said Miss May. She slumped down in her seat and Teeny and I followed suit. Miss May gestured at the building with her head. "Those people are going in."

I craned my neck a bit to get a look outside. Three twenty-something women knocked on the door three times, in a specific rhythm. The women were dressed in long, flowing dresses. Each wore a drowsy smile and their arms were all intertwined around each others' waists. After a few seconds, the steel door opened and the women went inside.

"Maybe it's not a cult," I said. *I mean, it was definitely a cult.*

Teeny sat straight up. "Chelsea. You saw those girls. Don't play dumb."

I hung my head. "Fine. This seems like a creepy, creepy cult and I don't wanna get involved."

Miss May took a deep breath and exhaled. "Whatever

the situation, those were young women. If Teeny and I go in there, we'll stick out like rotten bananas."

Teeny nodded fast in agreement. "That's true. Excellent point, May. We can't go in that cult. We would, of course... But the cult leaders would know right away that we're up to no good."

I grunted with resigned dismay. "You're saying I have to do this alone."

"You don't have to do anything you don't want to do." Miss May pressed a button on the dashboard and the rear passenger side door slid open with a slow creak. "But justice is on the line."

I shook my head. "Don't open that door on me. I'm not ready. What am I supposed to do in there? What are my goals? What room am I supposed to be in?"

"Calm down, Chelsea. Knock on the door," Teeny said. "Tell them you're a lost soul. Your fiancé left you at the altar and you need a place to stay."

"OK that's too personal," I said. "I have to actually confess my heartbreak?"

"The back story doesn't matter," said Miss May. "Just get inside that building, find Lillian's room and see if there's proof that she killed Beth."

I looked up and made eye contact with Miss May. "Oh well, when you put it like that... so easy!"

I took a deep breath to try and calm my nerves. I stepped out of the van and headed for the *All-Seeing Eye Communal Living Center.*

41

EYE SEE YOU

I knocked on the steel door just like the trio of girls had, with a simple but specific rhythm. Three knocks, each a little louder than the one that came before. After a few seconds, the door opened and I was face to face with an older woman. She had beautiful, gray hair down to her waist. She wore blue jeans and a long flannel shirt. And she gave me the warmest smile I had ever seen.

My first thought? *This is so annoying. Miss May and Teeny are definitely younger than this lady. I do not need to be here alone.* I resisted looking back at the van with a scowl as the woman held the door open.

"Greetings. Welcome. Come in."

The woman stepped aside and allowed me to enter a small brick foyer. The room was unadorned. There was an elevator on the far side. "Hi. Thank you for letting me in."

The woman nodded. "You look surprised."

"I am. I expected you to ask me questions or demand that I offer my qualifications for visiting your facility."

The woman let out a small chuckle. "If you are here,

you've been magnetized to our community, and that's enough of a qualification. *All-Seeing Eye* only attracts those who need us most."

"So you don't want to know my back story?"

The woman scoffed. "There are no back stories in life. Not like with characters in books or movies. We're living people. We are ongoing stories, evolving shapes. And as such, we must focus on the present and enjoy being rooted to the earth with every step we take. You need a place to stay for the night or longer?"

I stammered. "Yes. My husband... I was supposed to be married..."

The long-haired lady held up her hand to stop me. "No back stories. Only the present."

The woman crossed the room and pressed the button to call the elevator. I drifted behind her almost in a trance. It felt good to forget the past. But then the elevator arrived and I stepped inside, and I tried to snap back to my mission. As we glided up to the fourth floor I remembered that I was in that building for a reason. I needed to bring justice to Beth. I couldn't forget that, no matter how much I wanted to stay rooted in the present and the hypnotizing effect of the woman's voice and smile.

The elevator opened on the fourth and we stepped out into a large, loft-style living area. There were couches arranged in a circle. A cluster of women meditated along the back wall. Another older woman, who looked just like my host, cooked in the kitchen on the other side of the loft.

"Welcome," my host said, sweeping her arm across the space. "Living quarters are through the door at the other end of the room. Feel free to take any room that's open. If you'd like to rest, do so. If you crave connection and you'd like to meet any of your fellows, return to this room and I'll provide a proper introduction."

"Thank you. I mean it. This is all very nice."

The woman smiled and nodded. Once again, her smile comforted me. But I saw something vacant in her eyes. My hand shook as I worked up the nerve to cross the room. I took a deep breath, and headed back toward the living quarters.

I stepped out of the main loft area and into a long hallway lined with rooms. I glanced into each room as I walked by, trying to determine where Lillian might have been staying. Each room was small. Barely bigger than a closet. The rooms were all furnished with an identical twin bed, a small writing desk, and a flower in a thin vase. The warmth and comfort of the living area seemed a distant memory as I peered into the bare, claustrophobic rooms. I forced myself to keep walking even though the place was seeming more and more cultish.

About halfway down the hallway, I stopped. The room to my right had the same drab furnishings as the others. But there was a popcorn kernel on the floor and it looked sticky.

"Kettle corn," I muttered to myself. I looked behind me to make sure I was alone in the hall, then I stepped inside the room and closed the door.

The first thing I noticed once I was in Lillian's room was that there were no windows. The tiny bedroom was almost pitch black. I found a lamp on a bedside table and fumbled to turn it on. I picked up the lamp and wielded it like a candle, pointing it around the room to get a better look at my surroundings.

The place was extremely neat and tidy, other than that popcorn kernel. *Tidiness must be a rule of living in the cult*, I thought. I wondered if all residents were eventually forced to give up their personal goods. Because other than the furniture, Lillian's bedroom appeared empty. I looked under the bed, it was clean. I looked in the closet, where a row of plain clothes were neatly arranged. Then I turned my attention to the desk. Probably where I should have been looking all along.

The top drawer of the desk was stuffed with files, folders, and newspaper clippings.

All the newspaper clippings were twenty or thirty years old, but I couldn't find the unifying theme. Then I found a marble notebook with Lillian's name on the cover. It reminded me so much of the notebook that had been mailed to the farmhouse earlier in our investigation. I thought that the notebook might be proof that Lillian had been the sender of Beth's journal.

I opened the marble cover and saw that every single page was covered in hastily scrawled, manic notes.

All of the notes were about Beth's death. And a few questions appeared over and over...

"Who did this? Did Beth have enemies? Who wanted Beth dead?"

My breath caught in my throat as I turned another page. The name "Big Jim" was written at the top. Below Big Jim's name was another set of questions... "What's his real last name? Where was he really born? Need birthday. Need connection to Beth. Need motive."

My heart started doing cartwheels in my chest. "Oh my god," I muttered. "Lillian thinks Big Jim killed Beth. Lillian's not the killer. She's another sleuth!"

"What are you doing in here?" A stern female voice spoke up from the doorway. I turned back. It was the friendly old woman who'd greeted me. "This is someone else's room."

"I didn't... I didn't know this room belonged to anyone."

"This room belongs to Lillian Edwards," the woman said, her voice cracking. "At least it did. The police are here. Lillian was murdered in the center of town."

42

HUDSON AND POTOMAC

Detective Gary Potomac looked like a former high school quarterback. He was 6 1/2 feet tall, he had blonde hair and a barrel chest and hazel eyes. His was a striking presence. And I liked it.

I didn't like Detective Gary Potomac much as a person because he wouldn't let me leave the communal living facility until he questioned me. And since I was the "newest resident," Gary refused to question me until he got through everyone else in the house first.

I slumped against the wall near the kitchen at the back of the room and twiddled my thumbs as I waited. Death had a way of following me from month to month, from town to town. And honestly, I was feeling pretty beat down. And kind of longing for the familiarity of Detective Wayne Hudson's gruff demeanor and skeptical smile. I wasn't sure why Wayne had shown up previously in Blue Mountain, but now Potomac was presiding over the case of Lillian's slaying. Where did Hudson's domain end and Potomac's begin?

I felt more shaken up than usual by Lillian's death. For

one thing, I was pretty sure she was innocent, and she didn't deserve her fate. For another, it seemed a lot like Lillian was a fellow amateur sleuth... which reminded me that the stakes of investigating a murder were life or death.

I could have cried, and I mean really cried, as I sat there and thought about the state of my life. Germany was in Africa, I hadn't been sleeping in my own bed, I was stuck by myself in the living room of a cult, and I was about to be questioned by a strange detective about a murder. Plus, Beth and Lillian had both been murdered. These were two women who'd struggled with mental health issues and who'd likely been marginalized and overlooked their whole lives. Yes, they'd been difficult and confrontational people in my experience, but that was probably a reaction to years of strife and pain. Beth and Lillian had both needed help, and instead, they'd ended up dead. I hoped that their troubles were over now, and that they'd find each other again, in some better place, in some other life.

So yes, I definitely could have ugly-cried some big fat tears, but I didn't want to make a scene or draw attention to myself. And I knew I needed to stay calm for my conversation with Gary.

Gary's boots thudded on the ground as he approached me. I looked up, way up, and met his hazel eyes. "Ready for me?" I asked.

Gary reached down and offered me his hand. "I sure am. Let me help you up. Why don't we have a cup of coffee and talk?"

I took Gary's big, warm hand and got to my feet. Once I was standing, he adjusted his grip and shook my hand, then gave me a bright, white smile. "I'm Detective Gary Potomac. Good to meet you."

I let go of Gary's hand and wiped my palm on my jeans. *Yes, very sweaty*. "Good to meet you too, I guess."

"Right. Never pleasant to meet under these circumstances," he said. "I promise this won't take long."

Gary poured us both a cup of coffee and I took a seat on one of the couches at the front of the room. As we spoke, I did my best to answer his questions. Gary, unlike the woman who ran the commune, did require a back story. Remembering what Miss May had suggested back in the van, I told him my sob story about Mike leaving me at the altar. The truth was always easier than a lie, even when the truth was also kind of a lie. Gary believed every word I said. He shook his head when I told him about how Mike had stolen my interior business, and Gary let a big sigh when I finished speaking.

"I'm sorry you had to go through that." Gary sipped his coffee. "Please know that not all men are terrible."

I nodded. "I'll have to take your word for it," I said.

Gary chuckled and we made eye contact. *Oh no. Had I begun flirting? Listen, I may be sweaty and awkward, but I'm not immune to the charms of a handsome detective.*

I had a boyfriend, of course. But he was in Africa with the lions. And Gary was very much in America, present and in the moment. Nonetheless, I felt guilty. I put my coffee cup down on the table. "Am I free to go?"

Gary barely registered my question. He was looking off into the distance, forlorn. "You know, Lillian Edwards was incredible. Do you know her?"

I shook my head.

"I didn't know her very well, either. But this other woman got murdered over in Pine Grove. Her name was Beth. Lillian and Beth were great friends. When Beth died, Lillian took it upon herself to solve the mystery and catch the killer." Gary chuckled to himself. "I tried to stop Lillian from investigating the case. But she was determined and smart. She talked to everyone in town who might have had information. She was something else. You know, her murder is barely in my jurisdiction. I don't cover much of Blue Mountain. But we're right on the border here, so her death happens to fall to my department. I don't know if I should be happy or sad about that. Poor girl."

"Wow, I… I had no idea about any of that stuff," I said. I felt wobbly and surreal…that notebook in Lillian's room had in fact been evidence that she was an amateur sleuth, just like me. Gary Potomac was Lillian's version of Wayne Hudson.

"Do you want to know a secret?" Gary looked at me with a twinkle in his eye.

"Sure."

"I asked Lillian on a date. Just recently. There's a new pizza place in the village, I wanted her to go with me. She was playing hard to get. So we never had our date. But I think, eventually, she would have given me a chance. Everyone in this town saw her as some crazy, pathetic woman. But I knew the truth. Lillian was special. She didn't belong at *Five Pines*, and she didn't belong here."

I had a sudden pang of remorse about my coldness toward Wayne. I'd rejected him so many times, and I thought about how sad I would be if I never saw him again.

Remorse quickly gave way to fear, as I was again reminded of the similarities between myself and Lillian. Lillian had clearly been murdered because she was trying to find a killer. I'd had a few brushes with death myself, and any of those encounters could easily have turned fatal. Still, I didn't want Lillian's murder to deter me from the pursuit of justice. If anything, I wanted it to strengthen my resolve.

So when I emerged from the commune and headed back toward Miss May's van a few minutes later, I walked with strong, powerful steps.

A fellow sleuth had been murdered and I would not rest until her killer was found.

43

THE KEY TO THE CASE

I was so happy to be out of the cult, I practically dove back into the van — where Miss May and Teeny were both waiting with worried and expectant stares.

As the van door creaked closed behind me, Miss May and Teeny let out huge, simultaneous sighs. Teeny fanned her face with her hands. "Chelsea. I'm red in the face from nerves. What are the police doing here? Are you OK?"

I was OK, technically, but I didn't feel OK. I felt flustered and shocked and unsettled. I needed a moment to gather myself. Funny thing about having two caring, nosy best friends? You don't get a lot of moments.

"Chelsea. Snap out of it." Miss May craned her neck back from the front seat. "Are you OK or not? Tell us what happened."

I took a deep breath and tried to summon the energy to explain myself. Going "undercover" in the cult had demanded a lot of solo-sleuthing mojo. All that lying and sneaking around had given me a wild adrenaline rush, but now the adrenaline was rapidly bidding adieu to my body and I felt exhausted. "I'm OK. Alright. Nothing bad happened to me."

Miss May slumped over with relief. "Oh thank heavens. When those police cars pulled up, we almost barreled inside and blew your cover."

"I was halfway across the street when Miss May caught up to me and made me come back to the van," said Teeny. "She said you could handle yourself. I agree. But even karate queens need backup sometimes. Did you have to use your karate in there?"

"No karate chops or roundhouse kicks required. But Lillian's dead."

"She's dead?! Murdered?" Teeny asked.

"I think so. That's what I heard. That's why the cops are here."

"Well what are the details?" Miss May asked. "Tell us everything you know."

"Can we go home?" I asked. "I'll tell you on the drive."

"What do you mean home?" Miss May asked. "You want to go to Teeny's house for bed or do you need something back on the farm?"

I looked back at the cult. I thought of Lillian's small room. Her eulogy at the funeral. Her impatience at the bar. Her flight from *Five Pines.* Her struggle to solve the mystery of the murder, in spite of her own mental health issues.

Lillian had been a fighter. She'd fought against an unseen killer, against a system that marginalized the mentally ill, against her own demons... and in that moment, thinking about Lillian's courage and doggedness, I had a surge of strength.

I sat up a little taller in the backseat, and I cracked my knuckles for emphasis. "I don't want to sleep at Teeny's anymore," I said. "I don't want to be afraid of this killer.

Let's go back to the farm and spend the night in our own beds."

Teeny bit her lip. "That's not a good idea. The killer might have your keys, remember? That means they can break into your house and kidnap you or pour milk on you or do whatever they want at any moment."

"The milk thing seems weird," I said, "but the point is, I'm done living scared."

Miss May turned the keys in the ignition. "Let's talk about this later. But I'll head back to the farm for now. I need to set out the pies for tomorrow, anyway."

On the ride back over to the farm, I told Teeny and Miss May everything that had happened in the cult. Of course, my aunt and her friend had tons of questions and I did my best to provide answers. Miss May pressed for more information about Lillian's living quarters. But everything had blurred together. All the rooms had looked so similar. Normally, my interior design background gave me an eye for detail. But the homogeny of all of those rooms had almost created a blank composite in my brain. I remembered Lillian's notebook and not much else.

Teeny asked if the beds in the little rooms had been comfortable. Miss May and I joked about Teeny going to live with the women in the cult. But Teeny insisted she could never live in a place where she'd have to share a kitchen with a bunch of cult members who "probably didn't know the first thing about making hashbrown lasagna." We laughed.

After a few minutes, the conversation turned to an analysis of Lillian's theories on the murder, and if she could have been killed because she knew too much.

"What do you think, Miss May?" I poked my head up toward the front seat. "Does the notebook I found in Lillian's room make you think Big Jim is our primary suspect? Lillian seemed so convinced."

Miss May shrugged. "It doesn't make him less of a suspect, that's for sure."

"I think he definitely did it," said Teeny. "You can't trust a magician. They make their whole living on the promise that they can disappear and get out of handcuffs."

"We know, Teeny," said Miss May. "You had bad relationships with magicians. You have an unfair bias."

"It's not about my relationships," said Teeny. "Big Jim is a shady guy. I don't like him. You saw how he was flirting with me! Ha! What a sleaze. He killed Beth, I know it. Probably killed poor Lillian too."

"Lillian certainly seemed to think it was Big Jim," I said. "I want to believe she was right. But I know better than to trust an easy solution. We've followed plenty of bad leads in the past. We've questioned innocent people more than I'd like to admit. Poor Sudeer Patel and his family have had to deal with us on almost every investigation, and I don't think he would hurt a fly. His wife Kayla's gonna get a restraining order against us if we show up there again."

"Good point, Chelsea," said Miss May. "Lillian's suspicions don't necessarily mean Big Jim is the killer. And I'm not sure I understand what Big Jim's motive might have been."

Teeny turned back to me. "Did Lillian write down any potential motives in her notebook? Did she know why Big Jim might have killed Beth?"

I closed my eyes and thought back to the notebook. Images of Lillian's chicken-scratch handwriting sprung to my mind, but I couldn't recall any indications of motive. "I'm not sure," I said. "But I'll think about it."

A few minutes later, we entered the bakeshop to find KP

sitting at one of the tables eating an entire peach pie by himself. Steve the dog sat beside KP with a hungry look in his little canine eyes. Every so often, KP tossed Steve a piece of buttery pie crust and Steve gobbled it up off the floor.

"Hey KP," I said as we entered. "Peach pie for dinner?"

KP gave me a little grunt. "That's right." He returned back to the pie without making further conversation. KP was usually gregarious, but not when he was focused on his pie.

"There was another murder," I said, almost without emotion.

"Anybody I know?" KP asked.

"The woman who gave Beth's eulogy," I said.

"Yea, though I walk through the valley of the shadow of death, I fear no evil," KP said. "Amen."

I smiled sadly. KP's truncated recitation of Psalms 23 felt oddly poignant. We were all exhausted, and it showed in our muted response to this murder.

Miss May walked behind the counter to prepare for the next day. Teeny and I followed, and the three of us continued discussing the case.

"So we're not sure if we can trust Lillian's intel. We don't know if it was Big Jim." I helped Miss May arrange a few pies. "So who are our other suspects?"

"That's what I'm thinking about," said Miss May. "Are we sure Lillian couldn't have been the killer?"

I shrugged. "We don't have proof that she was innocent. But someone killed her — maybe for what she knew. Or, I guess it's possible... If Lillian did kill Beth, it's possible someone killed Lillian as revenge."

Teeny stepped forward. "Lillian's the one who purchased the Eternal Deck that we found at the scene of the crime. Which means she was the one who left that tarot spread."

“Eh, or was she? Big Jim claims Lillian bought those tarot cards,” said Miss May. “But I’m not sure we can trust his intel either.”

“I didn’t think of that, but you’re right.” I placed a pie in the display case and positioned it perfectly under the light. “It’s hard to trust Big Jim or Lillian. Lillian had mental health issues. We know that she was in an institution just last week. Maybe her theory was paranoid and delusional. Maybe Lillian killed Beth and then was overcome with grief and guilt so she built up a whole narrative about Big Jim being the killer to make herself feel better.”

Miss May shook her head. “I don’t know. That seems far-fetched to me. Will you pull a tub of butter out of the freezer? I need it to thaw for tomorrow.”

“OK.” I crossed into the kitchen, opened the freezer, and grabbed the butter. But something shiny caught my eye... “Oh my goodness. I found my keys.”

That’s right. I had left my keys in the freezer. I’d like to say I’d never done something like that before, but...

I rushed back into the bakeshop jangling the keys above my head. “My keys weren’t taken by the killer. I just left them in the freezer.”

Teeny and Miss May laughed. “Chelsea, Chelsea, Chelsea,” said Teeny. “I swear, you’d lose your ears if they weren’t connected to your brain.”

“I don’t think my ears are connected to my brain,” I said.

“You understand what I mean,” said Teeny. “Don’t be a know-it-all.”

“Hold on a second,” said Miss May. “If your keys were in the freezer, then how did the killer lock the door from the outside after they killed Beth?”

KP laughed with a mouth full of peach pie. “Oh yeah.

I've been meaning to talk to you girls about that. You don't need a key to lock that door from the outside."

The three of us turned to face KP. "Why not?" I asked.

"Yesterday I was working out by the peaches, thinking back to my days in the Navy. And I remembered you can lock the door from the outside pretty easy. There was a guy who taught me how to do it back in training camp. It's like picking a lock in reverse."

"I've never heard of that," said Miss May.

KP shrugged. "It's not hard. If you got the right tools, you can lock any door from the outside in just a few minutes. Especially on an old barn like this. It's not like this is the United States mint or anything."

Miss May pulled out a chair and sat down. "So the killer went through a lot of trouble to confuse us. But who? And why?"

I shrugged. "Maybe they locked the door from the outside to distract us from the other details of the crime."

"That's a decent theory," said Teeny. "We spent a lot of time thinking about how the door got locked and worrying about it. Heck, we were so scared about it that you two left the farm for days and slept in my house. I loved those slumber parties, but what if that's exactly what the killer wanted? To get you worked up about your own safety and to lure you away from the scene of the crime."

I scratched my chin. "The only reason we went to your house was because my keys were missing," I said. Then a thought occurred to me and I clasped my hands over my mouth. "Oh my goodness. What if I didn't forget my keys in the freezer? What if the killer found them and stashed them in the freezer to trick us?"

"It's certainly possible," said Miss May. "Although it's also very possible that you absent-mindedly left your keys in the fridge." She looked back over at KP. "Was Big Jim in the military?"

KP shrugged. "I think so. Not positive but sounds right."

Miss May turned back to me and Teeny. "Maybe Big Jim learned the same trick..."

I nodded. "Even if he didn't learn it in the military, he could have picked up the skill from a magic book or class, something like that. Sounds like something a magician would know how to do."

Teeny jumped to her feet. "What now? We go find that big stinky magician and get a confession?"

Miss May shook her head. "If we're going to accuse Big Jim we need more information. I don't want to be hasty or rash."

"And accusations can be dangerous," I said.

"Exactly," said Miss May. "Lillian seemed to think Big Jim was pretending to be someone he's not. I think she might have been onto something. So let's go find out." Miss May headed toward the exit and Teeny and I followed.

KP called after us. "Hey. No 'thank you?' No 'great job KP?' Sounds to me like I broke your case wide open!"

Miss May answered him without looking back. "The peach pie is your thank you," she said.

I heard KP laughing as he shut the door behind us. I giggled too, until I remembered that we were on the trail of a murderer.

And that was no laughing matter.

44

OFF THE RECORD

We waited until the next morning to make our next move in the case.

We didn't want to confront Big Jim yet, so instead, we went to visit Liz, the editor of the *Pine Grove Gazette*. Miss May had been gung-ho the prior night, energized by the revelation about my missing keys. But Liz hadn't picked up her office phone or home phone, so we had decided to hold off until the next day.

When we arrived at Liz's office, she was sitting at her desk, typing with hyper-focused fury. Each clack of the keyboard sounded like a gunshot. That girl could type, and I was suddenly glad I had never been in her journalistic crosshairs.

Liz didn't even notice when Miss May, Teeny and I quietly stepped into the room. After thirty seconds, Miss May cleared her throat. Liz did not look up from her computer. "Sit down. Typing. Emergency article. The news never sleeps, so neither do I." Liz grabbed a coffee mug from her desk and took a huge gulped. Coffee dribbled on her chin and she wiped it off with her sleeve, all without missing a keystroke.

"Were you working on a story last night?" Miss May settled into a chair opposite from Liz. "We couldn't get a hold of you."

Liz nodded. "Undercover assignment. I had to use a new alter ego to gain a foothold at the Department of Water and Power. There's something amiss at that place. A leaky faucet, if you will. I'm out to plug that leak."

Teeny raised her eyebrows. "Impressive."

"Impressive is an inadequate word for what I'm attempting. If all goes according to plan, this story will be monumental. It's going to be national news, and then maybe international news. I suspect that in six months if you travel to Brazil, China, or Japan, people will be talking about this story I'm writing here in front of you today."

I cocked my head to one side. "Just those three countries?"

Liz slammed her laptop shut. "Not just those three countries. The story is going to be global. Every country. Those were just examples. Please. Sit down."

Teeny and I obeyed, sitting at the chairs beside Miss May.

"I have five minutes. What's up?" Liz downed another big sip of coffee.

"Hold on one second." Teeny scooted to the edge of her chair. "Who's your new alter ego? I'm dying to know."

"I can't say. But I will say I've taken on the persona of a highly educated man. I will not share any of his physical characteristics and I will not tell you where he was born and raised. That's all you get. Four minutes and twenty-four seconds remaining."

Miss May launched into the story of our investigation.

She got around to the point quickly. We needed information about Big Jim. And we were hoping Liz could point us to some newspaper articles or town documents that might help us understand Big Jim's back story. Did he have a secret identity? Did Big Jim, himself, have an alter ego?

Liz listened with patience as Miss May spoke. Then she stood and slid her laptop into her bag. "I can't help you with this."

Miss May sprung to her feet. "Why not? You know everything that goes on in this town."

Liz stopped and look out the window. "Not ancient history like that. You want information from Jim's childhood, right? Well, he's an ordinary citizen, or he was back then, before he opened the magic shop. So he wouldn't have made the paper for any reason. And most of Pine Grove's birth/marriage/death records from that time were lost in a fire. Never digitized."

"There was a fire?" I asked.

Liz scoffed. "There were tons of fires. Back then, people didn't understand the meaning of 'flammable' or 'fire hazard.' Basically anytime somebody plugged in a toaster, there was a 50/50 shot they were gonna burn their house to the ground."

"There has to be some way you can help," I said.

"This might be the first time in my life that I can't be any help at all, Chelsea." Liz opened the door and stood aside for us to exit. "Now please get out. I need to wash last night's fortune cookie crumbs off my face, and I would rather do that in private."

We exited with our heads hung low. When we got back out to the car, I turned to Teeny and Miss May. "If Liz can't help us gather information, who can?"

Teeny's face lit up like a thousand-watt bulb. "I know! Ms. Happy! Is Ms. Happy still alive?"

Miss May nodded. "Alive and kicking."

45

THE SECRETS OF HAPPY-NESS

Ms. Happy was the oldest woman in Pine Grove. According to Miss May, Ms. Happy had been the very first resident of Pine Grove's retirement community, *Washington Villages*. If that were true, it would mean that Ms. Happy was well over a hundred years old when we went to see her.

Although I'd never been an ageist (my two best friends were thirty years older than me), I was skeptical that Ms. Happy would be a good source of information for the investigation. Somehow, a centenarian seemed bound to have forgotten some facts along the way. I mean, I left my keys in the freezer and I was a third of Ms. Happy's age. Nonetheless, we headed over to *Washington Villages* to find out what Ms. Happy knew about Big Jim and his origins in the area.

When we walked into the cafeteria of the retirement community, a large game of poker was going on at a circular table in the back. Miss May and I had visited that poker table on many prior investigations. Our frenemy Petunia was the head of the retirement community's gambling ring.

She always had information, and she liked to talk. But it was never fun to interrupt Petunia when she was in the middle of a game of Texas Hold 'Em.

Petunia turned from the card table and snarled at us before we had a chance to say a word. "What are you three doing here? Chelsea, are you still single? I would introduce you to one of my grandsons but they're all deeply in love with the women of their dreams. Beautiful families."

I stammered. Somehow I had forgotten Petunia's cutting sense of humor. "You know I'm not single anymore. I'm seeing Germany Turtle. He directed the town play?"

"Right. He weirds me out. Weird guy. Listen, you have my blessing but the kid is strange. And why is he named Germany? Who names their child after a country, and Germany no less? That's like naming your child Czech Republic or Yugoslavia."

"I don't think Yugoslavia is a country anymore," I said.

Petunia waved me away with an aggressive swat of the hand. "You know what I mean. Don't be a smarty-pants with me. You need me to help with one of your little investigations, right? Or are you here to accuse me of murder yet again?"

A curly-haired woman sitting across from Petunia at the table snickered. Petunia turned and snapped at her. "Don't you giggle over there. It's not fun to be accused of murder for no reason. If you're going to accuse me, at least accuse me of something I did. There are plenty of people I would murder if I had the chance. The mailman keeps bringing my packages two hours later than I need them. He'd be the first to go." Petunia chuckled. "I crack myself up. I'm sorry. Go ahead and laugh. I'm hysterical."

"I just have one question for you, Petunia," said Miss May.

Petunia looked up at Miss May like as if to say, "ask it already."

"What's Ms. Happy's apartment number?"

Ms. Happy lived in the most beautiful area of *Washington Villages*. Her apartment was nestled among tall trees and seated at the edge of a small pond. A cute stone walkway led to the front door and rosebushes lined the walkway.

"This is nice," said Teeny. "When I'm an old person, maybe I'll live here instead of at the cult."

Miss May turned to look at Teeny.

"I'm not old, May. Not old enough for a retirement community, at least. I have the hottest restaurant in town. Don't call me old."

Miss May chuckled and pressed the doorbell. The bell rang with a loud buzz.

"Wow. That's deafening," I said.

"It's probably a special buzzer so she can hear it. My mom has one of those." Teeny pressed the buzzer again. "I like the sound."

I heard the sound of shuffling feet from inside. Then the door opened and there stood one of the tiniest, most adorable women I had ever seen. She made Teeny look like a giant. Ms. Happy was 4'10", at most. She had enormous, thick bifocals. She was wearing a cute pink top with blue jeans and she had a bright, happy smile that suited her last name. She squinted at us when she opened the door. "Hello? Who are you?"

Miss May got reacquainted with Ms. Happy. They had apparently served on the town board together twenty years prior. When Ms. Happy finally remembered Miss May, she looked up with an even brighter smile and welcomed us into her home. We sat out in the back sunroom, overlooking the pond. Ms. Happy took approximately fifteen minutes to bring out a pitcher of iced tea. She refused our help, insisting she could do it herself. Then she sat down and we talked.

Ms. Happy's eyes widened when we told her about Beth's murder. "I can't believe it. Someone got murdered in Pine Grove? I never thought that would happen. Not in my entire life."

Miss May looked over at me, then back to Ms. Happy. "This isn't the first victim we've had in Pine Grove."

Ms. Happy lurched forward. "You can't be serious. Other people have been murdered in town?"

"Oh yeah," said Teeny. "If Pine Grove wasn't so incredible and adorable it might be a scary place to live."

"I don't get out much. Usually I stay in the living room. My best friend is ninety-seven and I'm a hundred and two. We gossip like we used to. She's not going to believe this. Although I wish you were here with better news."

"Hmmm. What's some other gossip? Chelsea has a boyfriend," said Teeny. "Her relationship history is complicated so it's good news that she found someone else to love her."

"Teeny's seeing someone too," I said. "Big Dan. He's the best mechanic in town."

Ms. Happy laughed. "That is good news. It's always good to have a mechanic you can trust."

"Also, Teeny's got another suitor, maybe you know him..." I said. "Big Jim, the local magician?"

Ms. Happy clucked her tongue at the mention of Big Jim. "I don't care for him."

"Is it possible he's not who he says he is?" I asked. "Could he have a dark past we don't know about?"

Ms. Happy took a long, slow sip of her iced tea. "I don't like talking about that man."

Teeny's eyes widened. "Why not?"

"He was a good boy, growing up. He mowed my lawn. He did a little magic show for my son's tenth birthday. Or maybe that was my nephew's birthday? The point is, I saw Big Jim do a magic show for children and he was friendly. Then Big Jim became a father and he showed his true character."

Miss May swallowed. "What do you mean?"

"Jim had three of the most adorable children I had ever seen. They were all born so close together. First came twin girls, then a little boy. No. It was twin boys, then a little girl. It was so nice seeing Jim and his wife and those three infants, all under two years old, walking through town on a Sunday. Then one day Jim left the family. Left the state. No one knew where he went."

"I knew I didn't trust that guy," said Teeny. "He disappeared on those poor kids."

Ms. Happy nodded. "That's right. He disappeared on those babies. As far as I know, the children were told their father abandoned them at birth. The kids never met their dad and he never got involved in their lives. Not even when they were growing up."

"That's so sad," said Miss May. "But I think you may have just given us information we needed to solve this case."

46

WHO'S YOUR DADDY?

"OK. So we think Big Jim was father to Michael, Jonathan, and Beth." I slid into my seat at our booth at *Grandma's*. Teeny slid in next to me and Miss May sat across from us.

Miss May nodded. "The more we talk about it, the more it seems obvious. Teeny was right about Big Jim. Even though she was generalizing about magicians. He abandoned his kids and now, all these years later, somehow that led to a murder."

"But how?" I asked. "Do you think Big Jim abandoned his kids and then killed one of them? I still don't see the motive."

"I don't see the motive, either," said Teeny. "But I do see a waiter." Teeny held up her hand. "Hey Samuel! Can you bring a platter of my famous puppies out?"

Samuel flashed a thumbs-up and Teeny turned back to us with a smile. "You always get good service when you own the place."

"We get good service here and we don't own the place. I think it's because you hire good people."

Teeny shrugged. "You got that right. I've got instincts. I proved that with Big Jim the stinky magician. What are you two talking about, motive, anyway? Trying to figure out why he killed his kid? Who needs a reason? He's a creepy, sneaky, evil magician."

"Slow down." Miss May held up her hand and Teeny stopped talking. "Let's just go through the facts."

I nodded. "So... What are the facts?"

"Beth was murdered at our farmhouse. There was a tarot card spread laid out in front of her when she died. The door to the bakeshop was locked from the outside when we found her."

I sighed. "It's a real mystery."

"Hold on," said Miss May. "I'm not done with the facts. "Big Jim abandoned his children when they were infants. Big Jim was also likely in the military in his youth. He may have learned how to reverse pick a lock in training camp just like KP. But how do we piece all this together?"

The waiter brought out a plate of hush puppies and set it down on the table. We each grabbed one and popped it in our mouths without saying a word. I had another hush puppy then got back to thinking.

"OK. Here's an important detail," I said. "Jim did not fully abandon his children."

Teeny scrunched up her face. "He didn't?"

I shrugged. "I don't think so. He came back to Pine Grove. When did he return to town, Miss May?"

Miss May shrugged. "A few years ago?"

"OK. So he disappeared when Michael, Jonathan, and Beth were children. They're all grown up now. So that means he was gone for at least thirty or forty years. Then he showed up a few years ago back in Pine Grove. What does that tell you?"

Teeny nibbled on a hush puppy. "I don't know. It sounds to me like he missed his hometown."

"It sounds to me like he was filled with regret," I said. "Big Jim abandoned his children, yes. We know that. He disappeared. But then he reappeared... maybe to try and make things right?"

"That makes sense," Miss May said. "Where you going with this? How does this lead to motive?"

"I'm trying to think about the whole scenario from the perspective of the children. Michael, Jonathan, and Beth were babies when their dad left. Being abandoned leaves you with psychological trauma. It's no wonder Beth grew up to have such faith in mystical arts like psychic readings and tarot cards. She had no sense of security at home. She had no father."

Teeny shook her head. "Those three kids are so strange. Growing up in that house must have been difficult."

I pointed at Teeny. "And that's the point I'm trying to make. These three fatherless children grew up in a sad, lonely home. The environment was probably tumultuous. I doubt the three of them got along. And Beth was a pariah. She was in and out of mental facilities. Her house was a disaster. I bet her brothers resented all the attention and care she demanded, as a kid and as an adult. Plus, her stints at *Five Pines* must have been expensive, and we know the brothers had money problems. They tried to get cash out of Salazar. They had overdue bills at their house. And they couldn't couldn't pay the funeral home after Beth's service. Maybe Beth had a life insurance policy, or maybe they just wanted her out of the way so they could stop being financially responsible for her."

"So are you saying..." Teeny waited for me to continue.

I nodded. "I think the Jenkins brothers teamed up and killed their sister."

"But I thought Big Jim was the killer," said Teeny.

"I don't think he would return to his home town, possibly to reunite with his estranged children, just to murder his daughter a few years later," I said. "It doesn't make sense."

Miss May chuckled. "Chelsea! You're stealing the show on this investigation. And I just thought of another detail that supports your theory."

Teeny leaned forward. "What is it?"

Miss May raised her eyebrows. "We got this clue all the way in the beginning of the investigation. But we missed it. We had everything we needed early on."

Teeny threw a hush puppy at Miss May. "Out with it. Now."

"OK," said Miss May. "I want the two of you to think back to the first time we visited the brothers at their home. There was an important piece of information there that we've been missing."

I closed my eyes and thought about that day. I thought about how one of the brothers had pulled on a gun on us, and I'd dismissed his hostility as too obvious. In retrospect, that had been foolish. "I mean, we were held at gunpoint, that should've been a sign..." I said.

"But that's not the clue," Miss May prodded.

Then it hit me. I opened my eyes. "Oh my goodness. The dry-cleaning."

"The dry-cleaning," said Miss May.

"The dry-cleaning?" Teeny said.

I turned to Teeny. "Remember the first time we encountered Jonathan and Michael? Jonathan came home with suits fresh from the dry-cleaner. They were black funeral suits."

Teeny threw up her hands. "So what? Their sister had just been murdered. They needed to look good for the funeral."

"Beth had only been murdered one night prior," I said. "I've never had dry-cleaning ready in under twelve hours. Have you? Has anyone?"

Teeny gasped. "Michael and Jonathan got their funeral suits dry-cleaned before Beth died. Because they knew she was about to die... Because they were going to kill her."

"That's right," Miss May said.

"I just got goosebumps," said Teeny.

"Me too," I said.

Miss May nodded. "So did I."

I took a deep breath and exhaled. "So what do we do now?"

Miss May slid out of the booth and stood up. "Now we go find those brothers before they kill someone else."

47

MISSION, IMPOSSIBLE

Our mission: to go to Michael and Jonathan's home and extract a confession for the murder of their sister, Beth.

Our vehicle: Teeny's hot pink convertible. Because why not?

I rode in the backseat and fidgeted nervously. I twiddled my thumbs, I twirled my hair, I scratched my ears...until I shoved my hands into my pockets and discovered a handful of cashews. *And if you're wondering, yes, I did eat a bunch of loose cashews from my jacket pocket.* I wasn't hungry, but I needed something to do to calm my nerves.

Teeny parked the car about a block away from the brothers' house so that we could retain the element of surprise. "Are you girls ready?"

Miss May set her jaw. "I'm ready. If we're right and these two are guilty, we get to have another peach party to celebrate the conclusion of another successful investigation."

"Can Peach come?" Teeny asked, referring to her aptly named sister. "She missed the last one and she's all worked up."

"Of course," Miss May said.

"I like the sound of that," I said, shoving more cashews into my mouth.

"Where did you get cashews?" Teeny asked.

"My pocket." I mumbled with my mouth full. "They're just OK."

"Oh Chelsea. How old do you think those are?" Miss May asked.

"It's not polite to ask a cashew its age," I said. "Let's just say old enough."

The three of us let out a simultaneous burst of nervous laughter. I rolled my shoulders to loosen up and tried to relax. Teeny looked back at me. "Are you getting limber in case you need to use your martial arts skills?"

I sighed. "I suppose. Although I hope these brothers roll over without a fight. They seem docile enough, don't they?"

"Not at all," said Miss May, "They seem like they have a lot of fight in them. And don't forget, we're here because we suspect they killed their own sister."

I hung my head. "Oh yeah. So are we just going to walk in there and say, 'We know Big Jim is your dad and we suspect you killed your sister because you're all messed up from when he left you and you're also broke?'"

Miss May shook her head. "We'll sort that out when we get in there."

"Yeah. We'll play it by our ears." Teeny yanked on both her ear lobes at the same time.

"I think the expression is, 'we'll play it by ear,'" I said.

"Well I want to use both my ears," said Teeny. "That's how they do it in Britain."

"Are you two ready?" Miss May opened her door and stuck a leg out onto the pavement. "I'll do the talking. Try to keep things peaceful. I've already got the recorder running on my phone to capture the confession."

I nodded. "Let's go."

The three of us walked down the street in a small triangle formation with Miss May at the front. We held our heads high and walked with long, powerful steps. At least Miss May and Teeny did. I tripped over my own feet two times between the car and the house. Just getting out my pre-accusation jitters.

When we arrived at Michael and Jonathan's house there wasn't a single light on in the entire home. And there were no cars in the driveway. Miss May ran her tongue along the inside of her cheek, thinking. "They're not home. Or they're pretending they're not home."

"What should we do now?" Teeny asked. "A little more breaking and entering? Chelsea's pretty good at climbing trees and flopping onto roofs."

Miss May pointed toward the front porch. "I don't think flopping will be required this time. The front window is open a crack."

"Let's do it," said Teeny, walking toward the front door.

I caught Teeny by the arm. "Wait... What if this is a trap? What if they're going to sabotage us?"

She put her hand on her head. "Good point. You should go first."

I looked from Teeny over to Miss May. Seemed like I was going first.

The front window slid open without making a sound. That time, I did not flop into the house. I climbed in like a verified cat burglar, with grace and elegance. Landed right on my feet. Seriously. I didn't even slip and fall because of extraneous sweat. It was one of my finest moments.

I opened the front door and Miss May and Teeny joined

me in the foyer. "Good job, Chelsea." Miss May put her hand on my elbow. She whispered. "Any signs of life?"

I shook my head. I hadn't seen anything. "No signs of death, either."

"Maybe they just happened to go on vacation," said Teeny.

Miss May shrugged. "Let's look around and see what we can find."

We stuck together as we searched the house. The last time we'd been to the house Beth shared with her brother's, it had been filthy and in disarray. This time, the place was clean. Every room greeted us with spotless surfaces and the smell of bleach hung in the air. Only a few items of clothing hung in the closets and someone had cleaned the refrigerator of all its food. (Teeny found that out when she opened the fridge to look for a snack.) When we had completed the search, we all three sat at the kitchen table.

"This is so strange," I said. "The brothers are long gone. The house is spotless. If they're going on vacation, it's a permanent vacation to a country with no extradition."

Miss May sighed. "It does appear Michael and Jonathan are on the run, as they say."

"They did such a good job cleaning this house," said Teeny. "I wish my staff at *Grandma's* would be this thorough with their cleaning. I'm always having to vacuum after they already said they vacuumed. Attention to detail goes a long way."

I nodded. "These two have excellent attention to detail. That's probably how they evaded our suspicion for so long. I mean, even though one of them did pull a gun on us... But they really led us on a wild goose chase with all these different clues. Think about that crime scene. Not a single item was out of place. Everything was so precisely laid out. So meticulous. So many misleading signs."

Miss May nodded. "It was premeditated, that's for sure." Miss May pulled out her cell phone and started to dial.

"Who are you calling?" I asked.

"The police. We have no idea where the brothers are. We don't have the technology to track them. I think we need to turn this investigation over."

Teeny slumped over. "Are you serious? We can't give up. We never give up."

"I'm not giving up. I'm sharing information and asking for help."

Miss May pressed her phone to her ear and walked into the front room to talk to the police. Teeny and I sat in shocked silence. Neither of us felt ready to hand this mystery off to the cops. We'd never acquiesced an investigation before, and I wasn't eager for that to change.

Miss May charged back into the kitchen a few minutes later, shaking her head. "Unbelievable. Unbelievable. I can't understand that woman."

I stood up. "What happened? You talked to Chief Flanagan?"

Miss May laughed with incredulity. "Yes. We had a wonderful conversation. I told Flanagan everything we learned. She acted like she knew all the information about Big Jim and the kids he abandoned and the brothers' debt. She just let me babble for five minutes straight. Then when I finally stopped talking Flanagan laughed at me."

Teeny huffed in disbelief. "Excuse me?"

"Yeah," said Miss May. "Flanagan said that the Pine Grove Police Department doesn't have the resources to chase all of our 'bogus leads.' She said that if the police investigated everyone we suspected, half the town would be in jail. She forbade me from continuing our investigation and told me we'll all go to jail for a long time if she caught us trying to solve this murder."

"So what now?" I asked.

Miss May crossed her arms. "Now we try to solve this murder."

48

THE BROTHERS GRIM

Spurred on by Miss May's newfound conviction, we hurried over to Big Jim's magic shop. No surprise, his place was also locked up. Teeny suggested we break in, but Miss May refused. The outside of the shop was littered with security cameras. Perched on the corners of the roof, the cameras reminded me of waiting vultures. A large sign on the front door warned, "Fortress Security Systems: Intruders Beware."

As we trudged back to the car from the magic shop, it was my turn to feel defeated. "The brothers grim and their deadbeat dad have disappeared on us. Like an illusion in a magic show. Or... like a deadbeat dad. We're a step behind. How did we let this happen? We're usually a step ahead."

"Chelsea, no," said Miss May. "Stop thinking like that. I had a moment of doubt back at the brothers' house and that's enough doubt for the three of us. We solve murders. That's what we do. We've already completed the hard part of this investigation. We have our top suspects. Now all we have to do is find them."

"I like that attitude, May," said Teeny. "You're better at

this than Mr. Flowers. You're tall, confident, and driven. You won't back down. Mr. Flowers backs down all the time. He always needs to go get tea right in the middle of the investigation and sometimes he gets so tired he needs a nap."

"Your favorite murder investigation show includes scenes where the lead detective takes naps?" I asked.

Teeny nodded. "It's British. British TV takes its time. I like the napping scenes. Sometimes I nap, too."

"Enough Mr. Flowers," said Miss May. "Let's get back to the farmhouse to regroup. Maybe have some tea. It's getting late and we need to figure out our next move."

Teeny sped over to the farmhouse with a smile on her face. Miss May sat in the front seat with a hard, determined glare. I sat in the back, feeling nervous. I vacillated between wanting more cashews and wondering if those cashews might've gone bad. I felt a little queasy.

My queasiness intensified when we pulled up to the farmhouse and saw Big Jim sitting on the front steps with his head in his hands.

He stood when he saw us arrive.

Uh-oh. I definitely felt queasy.

49

DON'T MESS AROUND WITH JIM

"That guy looks like Big Jim," Teeny exclaimed. Dusk was upon us, and Big Jim was partially shrouded in the haze of the evening.

"That guy is Big Jim, Teeny." Miss May craned her neck to get a better look at him. Big Jim stood akimbo in the bright glare of Teeny's headlights. His shadow stretched for miles behind him. His eyes were barely visible. The whole scene gave the feeling that he might just POOF! and disappear in the dusty beams of light.

"He's not moving," Teeny said. "He's just standing there like a magician in headlights."

"We can see that, Teeny." Miss May grabbed her door handle. "I think we should get out and talk to him."

"I'm not so sure about that," I said. "He might be guilty. I mean, I know we decided it was the brothers. But Big Jim has lied to us. And he's acting shady. I don't trust him."

"You think a father killed his only daughter?" Miss May asked.

I shrugged. "I don't know. What if she wasn't even really

his daughter? What if we drew the wrong conclusions? I'm not sure of anything anymore."

"Well we're not gonna get more sure by sitting in the car," Miss May said.

Jim called out to us. He held up both his hands up to try to demonstrate that he didn't mean any harm.

"What is he saying?" asked Teeny.

"I couldn't hear him," I said.

"Me neither," said Miss May. "Put the windows down. Or the top."

Teeny nodded and rolled the windows down. She stuck her head out the window and squinted toward Big Jim. "What was that? We couldn't hear you."

"I said I'm sorry," said Big Jim. "I shouldn't have lied to you about the tarot cards."

Teeny looked back at me and Miss May. "He said —"

"We can hear him now," said Miss May. Miss May stuck her head out her window. "Empty your pockets."

Big Jim nodded. With slow and cautious movements he turned the pockets of his jean shorts inside out. He wasn't hiding a weapon anywhere. "Can we talk? I want to help the investigation."

"You stay right there," said Miss May. "We'll talk like this."

"I'm not dangerous," said Big Jim. "I just showed you. I don't have a gun or a knife or even any tricks up my sleeve."

"Doesn't matter what you showed us," said Teeny. "We don't trust magicians in this car. You people are all sneaky weirdos."

"That's not fair," said Big Jim. "That's a wild generalization."

"Just tell us why you're here," said Miss May. "Stop defending magicians, we all know they can be creepy. Some of them are very nice, I know, but Teeny has dated a few of you so she has some preconceived notions."

I stuck my head out the window. "Yeah!" *OK. Not my wittiest remark ever but we were in the middle of a tense moment.*

"Tell us what you know," said Miss May.

"I think you've already learned the truth about me," said Big Jim. "Michael and Jonathan are my sons. Beth was my daughter. I left them with their mother when they were babies. Walked right out on my family. Worst mistake I ever made."

"You should be ashamed of that," said Teeny.

"I am. Trust me, I am. Those three had it hard growing up. They're unique children. They didn't do well in school and their mother was...strange. The kids basically raised themselves. I'm sad to say, I'm not sure they did a very good job. I returned to Pine Grove to make amends. But I was too late. Michael and Jonathan have serious issues. If you suspect they killed their own sister...I'm sorry to say you're correct."

"We're always correct," said Teeny. "You can't get away with murder in this town. Or in the adjacent, smaller towns either!"

Big Jim nodded. "I felt terrible when I realized what my boys had done to Beth. I can't say I understand it, but I do understand that I'm to blame, at least in part. While I was relaxing and living the good life in Jacksonville, Florida for the past thirty years, those kids were struggling without a dad."

"You ran away to Jacksonville, Florida?" I asked. "Why?"

"I saw a commercial for Jacksonville on television. It seemed like paradise and it was."

Teeny scoffed. "Jacksonville is not my idea of paradise. If

you're going to live in Florida you need to be on the Gulf Coast."

"I visited the Gulf here and there. Spent some time in the keys. Not much of a Key West guy, to tell the truth."

"OK," said Miss May. "Keep telling us about your sons and Beth."

"Right," said Big Jim. "I felt responsible when I realized my sons had hurt Beth. I felt even worse when I realized that the three of you were going to catch them and put them in jail for life. I know it was wrong for them to kill Beth but I didn't want them to be punished for my mistakes. So... I started interfering in your investigation. First, I set up the tarot card spread and locked the door. Then I led you to Sudeer, then to Lillian Edwards to distract you from my boys. I also sent that notebook."

"And you pointed to yourself as a suspect so we'd never suspect you..." I said, putting things together as Jim spoke. "Smart. You really thought it through."

"If you want your sons to get away with this murder, why are you here?" Teeny asked.

Big Jim hung his head. "I'm here because... I was a bad father, yeah. But there are plenty of children who grow up without fathers. And most of those children do not murder their own sister in cold blood. My sons should be held accountable for what they did. I want to help hold them accountable. Because that's what a good father would do. A good father doesn't let his children get away with murder."

Sitting there, looking at Big Jim, I pitied him. This whole story — the absentee father, the lonely, strange children — it had an air of operatic tragedy. I noticed Big Jim's long, quavering shadow, and I thought about how the past follows us all around. Some of us figure out how to live with our mistakes, but some of us never do.

"How can you help us now?" I asked.

Jim let out a long, deep sigh. "I know where Michael and Jonathan are hiding. They plan to fly to South America in the morning. But if we go now, we can catch them before they leave."

"You want to take us to your sons? Turn them in?" Miss May bit her lip as she awaited Big Jim's answer.

Big Jim nodded. "Just promise you won't hurt them."

"We won't hurt them unless they try to hurt us," said Miss May.

Jim nodded. "They won't try to hurt you. I promise."

50

REUNITED

We told Big Jim we'd follow him to the secret location. He agreed to stay below the speed limit and not run any yellows. Then he jumped in his flashy sedan and set off, driving south on the Taconic State Parkway.

Big Jim had told us the brothers were holed up somewhere in New York City. We drove behind, weaving in and out of lanes, for about two hours. Then we found ourselves double-parked on a side street in the Washington Heights neighborhood of New York City. Big Jim parked one car-length in front of us, rolled down his window, and motioned for us to approach.

"This must be the place," said Miss May.

"Should we get out of the car?" Teeny asked.

Miss May shrugged. "If we don't get out of the car, there's no reason to have followed Big Jim here in the first place."

Miss May climbed out and walked toward Big Jim's vehicle. Teeny and I followed, lagging a step or two behind. Miss May stopped a safe distance from Big Jim's window and crossed her arms. "Alright. We came all the way down here. Now what?"

Big Jim pointed at the five-story brick building across the street. "That's the *Washington Heights Hotel*. The boys are in there. Room 502."

Miss May looked up at the fifth floor. "OK. Is there any reason they might know we're coming?"

Big Jim shook his head. "Is there any reason to believe the three of you might've called the police?"

Miss May shook her head. "We've learned from experience... police don't respond well to random murder theories. Pine Grove PD would never investigate in Manhattan. Manhattan police wouldn't listen to us even if we did call them. It is up to the three of us to get your sons to turn themselves in."

Jim raised his left eyebrow. "You mean the four of us."

Miss May shook her head. "Oh no. You're staying parked out here. Or you can drive back to Pine Grove, if you want. Either way, you're not going up there."

"I really think it would be better if I came with. Those boys will listen to me."

"They'll listen to us, too," Miss May said. "And so will you." Big Jim grunted and climbed back into his parked car.

The lobby of the hotel smelled musty and wet. The place looked like it had been fancy once, maybe in the 1920's. But under current ownership, it was the opposite of fancy. I might even go so far as to say, disgusting. The tiles were filthy. The granite receptionist desk was chipped and scratched. An angry young woman stood behind the counter looking even worse for wear than her surroundings.

"Hi. Just visiting a friend in room 502. Can you point us to the elevators?" Miss May used her polite, friendly voice.

It did not work on the disgruntled woman. "No elevator. Take the stairs."

Miss May blinked in confusion. "I'm sorry. Is there maybe a service elevator or a freight elevator? Five stories is a lot for these old legs."

The woman shrugged. "No elevator. Take the stairs."

Five stories was a lot for all of our legs. We stopped every flight to catch our breath. Sometimes, we stopped twice in one flight. But after about fifteen minutes we made it all the way up to the fifth floor. The stairway had been so grimy and repulsive, I sighed in relief when we stepped out into the hallway, even though it was also grimy and repulsive.

"This is what they call a two-star motel," said Teeny. "But I'm not sure how these places get those two stars. Maybe they bribed the reviewers. I'd give this negative five stars. Heavy marks off for how often I found myself wondering, 'Is this a blood stain or food?'"

Miss May gestured down the hall. "There's room 502. Ready?"

I took a deep breath and nodded. Teeny nodded too, so vigorously I thought her head might pop off. "I was born two weeks early. But even then, I was ready."

Miss May knocked on the door three times with her big, powerful fists. A nervous male voice called back. "Who is it?"

"Complimentary fresh-baked cookies from the kitchen," said Miss May.

Miss May looked over at me, proud. She always knew how to use baked goods to her advantage. "Do you really have cookies?" I whispered.

Miss May scrunched up her face. "Yes. But they're not for these two. They're for us on the drive home."

A few seconds later, the door opened to reveal the short, bald brother, Jonathan. His eyes widened when he saw us. "Wait. You don't work here."

Miss May stepped in the hotel room and Teeny and I followed. "You're right. We don't work for this hotel. But we need to talk." Miss May closed the door behind her.

Jonathan scrambled to get in front of us. His eyes darted around the room, as if he was searching for an exit. "I don't want to talk to you. I want you to leave. If you don't, I'm calling security."

Miss May chuckled. "This place doesn't have security, Jonathan. And it doesn't have a kitchen or staff that brings fresh-baked cookies to your door."

Jonathan looked down. "I thought that sounded too good to be true."

"I want you to go to your window, look down, and tell me what you see." Miss May pointed to the window across the room.

Jonathan edged toward the window, keeping one eye on us the whole time. "OK." He parted the blinds and looked outside. "I don't see anything. It's the street."

"See that nice car parked right in front of the hotel?" Miss May asked.

Jonathan turned back and winced. "Oh. You talked to my dad."

Miss May nodded. "He talked to us. Told us all about what you and Michael did." Miss May turned around. "Where is your brother, anyway?"

"Big Jim. That no-good, deadbeat, son of a... I can't believe he ratted me out! He told me he was sorry for leaving us. He told me he was going to keep you three away. I thought he was going to fix everything."

"A good father holds his children accountable for their actions," Teeny repeated. "Especially when his sons are murderers."

"You and your brother killed your sister. Then you killed Lillian Edwards. Those actions have consequences." I took a step forward and held my shoulders back. My hope was that my strong posture would remind Jonathan of my famous karate skills and convince him to back down without a fight. I wasn't sure word of my famous karate skills had even reached Blue Mountain, but still... I was doing my best to intimidate.

"You're wrong about that," said Jonathan. "I didn't kill Lillian Edwards."

A loud voice boomed from the doorway. "I did."

We spun back to the door. Big Jim stepped inside, closed the door and locked it behind him. "Big Jim," I said. "We should have known not to trust you."

"Magicians!" Teeny grumbled with disdain.

Miss May shook her head. "I thought you felt bad, Big Jim. You wanted to make things right."

"That's ridiculous, May. I'm not sending my own son to jail for murder. Beth was crazy. She thought everyone was out to get her, including me, and she couldn't hold a job. She was in mountains of debt. Yes, she was my daughter, but there was nothing but bad blood between us. She seemed to have bad blood with everybody. Even you, Chelsea. She thought everyone wanted her dead. In a way, Jonathan put her out of her misery."

"She was still a person," I said. "That's no way to talk about—"

Suddenly, Jonathan rushed at me and tackled me to the ground. We hit the gross, carpeted floor with a resounding thud.

"Get off me!" I tried to push Jonathan away but he was too short and stocky. His center of gravity was low and he was dense, so I couldn't budge him. Teeny lunged across the room and jumped on Jonathan's back. He flung her off like she was nothing more than a mosquito. Teeny hit the wall and slid to the floor, like a character from a comic book. "Ouch! You slimy little creep! That hurt."

Teeny got back to her feet, and Big Jim laughed. "We may be creeps, but somehow I don't think you three ladies are going to be able to defeat us."

"That's where you're wrong, Jim," said Miss May. She took two steps toward Jonathan and pulled her fist back, ready to deliver a punch. I'd never seen Miss May punch anyone, and I was kind of excited to witness my aunt fighting. Although her form was... not good.

Before Miss May could bring down the hammer, Big Jim caught her by the wrist and tossed her back toward the door. I struggled to stand so I could help Miss May, but Jonathan still had me pinned to the ground. His hand reached for my throat, and I felt his fingers closing around my neck.

Big Jim grabbed Miss May with one hand and Teeny with the other, and roughly shoved them into the bathroom. He slammed the door shut and propped a chair against the handle. Teeny and Miss May pounded and yelled, but they couldn't get out.

My eyes widened. Miss May and Teeny were indisposed. I was seconds away from losing my air supply. And I was outnumbered two-to-one by a murderer and his deadbeat dad, who, as it turned out was also a murderer. In all of our investigations, I had never been in this kind of immediate danger. In that moment, I forgot all my karate training and instead, resorted to pure instinct. I scratched at Jonathan's face. I attempted to scream for help but my voice was hoarse and muted by lack of oxygen.

I continued to struggle, kicking and hitting and thrashing, but I was starting to feel fear, real, cold fear... Fear that Jonathan's angry, squat face would be the last thing I ever saw.

Then came three strong knocks at the door to the room. "Police. Open up."

I choked out a single word: "Help."

"Open the door. Now!" A strong, angry voice demanded from outside.

Miss May and Teeny screamed from the bathroom. "Just come in. The killers are in here. We need help."

Crash. A black boot kicked through the door and three police officers stormed inside. In seconds, they had Big Jim in handcuffs against the wall. Then they pulled Jonathan off of me, slammed him against the wall and cuffed him too.

The cops let Miss May and Teeny out of the bathroom. We all looked at each other, in shock and relief. That had been a really close call, and we all felt shaken.

"It's OK." Miss May hugged me closer to her. "You're safe now. We're safe. It's OK."

"You're all safe," said someone from behind us.

Miss May let me go. We turned toward the sound of the voice. It was Michael, emerging from the closet. He had dark circles under his eyes. Like he hadn't slept in days, and he'd cried for forty-eight hours straight.

"Michael..." Miss May stepped toward him. "You called the cops?"

He nodded. "My brother... my father... I knew what they'd done, but they promised it was over. Then when I saw them trying to hurt you, I knew they had to be stopped."

I trembled as I thought about how easily things could

have gone a different way. If Michael hadn't been there, if the cops hadn't shown up right when they did...

But Miss May was right. We were safe. And we had caught another killer.

Actually, we had caught two.

And that meant it was time for a celebration.

51

BIG JAMES AND THE GIANT PEACH

At the end of every investigation, we hosted a celebration for the people of Pine Grove. Our "justice is served" bashes had become a much-anticipated tradition in town, and this time was no different.

It felt good for me, Teeny, and Miss May to let off a little steam after a stressful investigation. The same was true for the people of Pine Grove. Even if they hadn't immersed themselves in the mystery like the three of us had, they needed something uplifting after tragedy. A reminder that life was still good, and our community was still whole, and everybody could still find joy in being together on a warm summer night.

That Saturday was a beautiful, hot August day, so we decided to hold the event in the field beside the barn. I woke up early in the morning to set up the tables with classic red and white tablecloths. Miss May and I baked at least fifty peach pies for the partiers. KP spent the whole afternoon rigging up a sprinkler system for the local kids to run through as a respite from the heat.

By six o'clock, the party was jumping. Tom Gigley and

his band *The Giggles* played a funky version of Bruce Springsteen's "Born to Run." Petunia and her poker buddies/victims savored slices of peach pie at a table as they played a casual game of Omaha Hi-Lo.

Steve the dog limped around from one table to another, getting lots of attention as people marveled at his incredible cuteness. KP followed Steve around, making sure the dog behaved and rewarding the canine with an occasional chunk of buttery crust.

I realized suddenly that there was still one mystery left to solve — the missing peach pie from the bakeshop. I grinned as a lightbulb went off in my head.

"KP!" I called out. "Hey, KP. I have a question." KP strolled over to me, Steve limping along right on KP's heels.

"What?" KP grunted affably.

"Do you happen to know if a particular limpy little dog might've burglarized the bakeshop on the night of Beth's murder?"

KP shook his head. "Hmm. If you're implying that Steve here devoured an entire peach pie and I helped him cover it up so he wouldn't get in trouble with Mabel, well, you're wrong. I don't know what happened to that missing pie, and neither does Steve."

Steve barked in agreement.

"OK," I said. "I guess some mysteries are better left unsolved."

KP muttered in agreement, and walked back into the barn. I watched them go, a conspiratorial smirk spreading across my face. I'd forgotten about the missing pie as a clue, but seems it may have been a red herring anyway. A delicious red herring that got eaten by a dog.

I was pouring myself a glass of fresh peach sangria when Sudeer approached me. "Solved another one, didn't you?"

"Hey, Sudeer."

"How's the sangria?"

I handed him my glass. "Try for yourself. I'll pour another one."

He took a sip and smiled. "Wow. You and Miss May should bottle this and sell it."

I chuckled. "Maybe we will. By the way, I'm sorry we suspected you of murder again. I mean, we didn't really suspect you. But we came to question you. I mean, not really question you, just talk. You know what I mean. "

"Don't worry about it," Sudeer said. "You can question me every time as long as you keep finding the real criminals in Pine Grove. It's kind of fun, being a regular in your cases."

I gave Sudeer a friendly nod and headed over to my table. People crowded the dance floor, moving and grooving to *The Giggles'* funky cover songs.

I was tempted to join, but my feet hurt and I was already sweating from that glass of sangria. The investigation into Beth's murder had been more stressful than our other mysteries. Realizing the danger of solving murders reminded me how risky our hobby was, and left me feeling introspective. Grateful to be alive, but also pensive and a little somber.

Nonetheless, I relaxed as I settled down at my picnic table. Teeny was there with Brian, the owner of the local coffee shop. She was telling the story of our finale back in the motel with glee, reenacting every move with broad, sweeping hand gestures. Brian was so shocked, his eyes were practically bugging out of his head. "You have to be kidding me," he said. "Did it really go down like that, Chelsea?"

I sighed. "I wish I could tell you she was making this stuff up. But it was real."

Master Skinner, my karate sensei from childhood, piped up from nearby. "I heard you were almost bested, Chelsea."

I looked down. "That's right, Master Skinner."

"If you'd ever like to brush up on your skills, learn how to break free of any hold, the dojo is always there for you."

"Thanks," I said.

Teeny perked up. "Oh. Can I come? I need to learn karate, too. As a member of the Miss May and Chelsea crime-solving team, I have to be able to protect myself."

"It would be my honor to teach you self-defense, Teeny," Master Skinner said with a small bow. "I have learned, over the course of my studies, that small stature can be an asset in martial arts if wielded with confidence."

Master Skinner walked away, and I chuckled as I watched him go. "Pine Grove is lucky to have such a dedicated sensei," I said.

"Not as lucky as we are to have you," a male voice said.

I looked over my shoulder.

Wayne was standing behind me, a small smile creeping across his stoic face. "Hi, Chelsea. Can we talk?"

52

PEACHES AND DREAMS

Wayne strolled off through the peach trees and I walked beside him. He moved slowly, as though considering every step he took. So did I.

When he finally spoke, his words were measured and drawn out. "So. You solved another mystery."

I looked back at the party happening behind us. The sounds drifted through the heavy summer air, the muted notes of some Van Morrison cover and the muffled din of tipsy chatter. "Yeah. Are you tired of being out-investigated by an interior designer and her elderly aunt yet?" I didn't mean to flirt, but it may have seemed like I was flirting.

Wayne smiled. "I heard the showdown was dangerous. You went in there without the police."

"We didn't have much choice. Anyway, I don't really need a lecture right now about—"

Wayne held up his hand. "Hold on. That's not what I'm doing. Not at all. I mean, of course I want you to be careful. But it takes real courage to do what you did. I admire that."

I looked down. "Oh."

Wayne reached up and pulled a leaf off the tree. "I've

always admired that about you. Let me ask... what was up with the tarot cards?"

"Big Jim put them there. To confuse us. He wanted to send us on a wild goose chase, and it worked."

"Well, at least you three wild geese ended up solving a complicated murder," Wayne said. "I'm impressed."

I blushed. How had I gotten here, standing in the early moonlight among the peach trees with Wayne? It was all too romantic. I had a boyfriend. In Africa, yes. But still. He existed. I had assumed Wayne wanted to talk about the case in a more straightforward manner. I tried to pivot back to that. "You know, Flanagan is a bad police chief. We tried to tell her about the brothers and she just ignored us."

Wayne looked over at me. "I didn't hear about that."

I nodded. "Yeah. Miss May called the PGPD and told Chief Flanagan everything. Flanagan told Miss May that it was a waste of time for the Pine Grove police to pursue our theories."

Wayne shook his head and put a hand in his pocket. "Unreal. Chief Flanagan is my superior officer, so I'm not going to say anything disparaging about her. I will say, however, I might have handled the situation differently. You and Miss May and Teeny have solved enough murders to earn a little bit of credibility around here."

"Just a little?" I said, with a smirk. *Shoot! I was flirting again.*

Wayne rolled his eyes. "OK. A moderate amount of credibility."

I pressed my hand into the bark of a tree. The rough, mossy texture felt good on my skin. "I used to climb these trees when I was a kid. I spent entire afternoons up in these branches, reading books or listening to music."

"These are beautiful trees." Wayne placed his hand on

the bark, not close enough to touch but close enough for me to feel guilty about the proximity. He looked over at me. "Really beautiful."

Oh no. What was happening? Was Wayne calling me beautiful using a thinly veiled tree compliment?

Wayne removed his hand from the bark and I breathed a sigh of half-relief, half-disappointment. He looked down and brushed the tree residue from his palms.

I swallowed, then spoke, barely above a whisper. "Why did you want to talk to me?"

Wayne looked at me. Our eyes met. Neither of us spoke for a long moment, and then his lips parted. *To talk? To kiss me? What was about to—*

"Chelsea." A familiar voice broke the moment. I turned. It was Germany Turtle, smiling and wearing his usual get-up of jeans, a denim shirt, and a denim jacket.

"Germany! What are you doing here?" I asked.

"Yeah," Wayne said. "I thought you were in Africa."

"I heard you solved another mystery. I wanted to return to congratulate you on serving yet another plate of cold justice."

I giggled. Germany had such an unusual way with words. Germany rushed toward me and wrapped me in his denim-clad arms. Maybe I was imagining it, or maybe Wayne tensed up as Germany hugged me closer.

"All the lions in Africa couldn't keep me away from you, Chelsea. Unless of course, I was attacked by a pride. Suffering a physical, lion induced injury would likely keep me in Africa and away from you. However, it's just an expression. I hope you get my meaning."

"I think she gets it," Wayne said with a soft chuckle. Even Wayne couldn't help but be amused at Germany's quirkiness.

"Detective Hudson. Greetings." Germany reached out and shook Wayne's hand. *Was it just me or did Wayne squeeze a little too hard?*

Germany withdrew his hand from Wayne's grip and turned back to me. "I requested a special song from the band. Will you join me for a dance?"

I glanced back. Wayne gave me a small smile. "Have fun. I'm going to climb this tree and read a book."

I averted my eyes. "The top branch is stronger than it looks. Don't be afraid to climb high."

Wayne smiled. "I never am."

Germany took my hand and led me away from the peaches. As we walked, I thought back on the investigation. I remembered Beth accusing me of wanting to kill her. I remembered hiding behind the shed at Salazar's house. And I remembered the waiter at *Grandma's* unveiling Teeny's precious hushpuppies. The investigation into Beth's murder had been a strange blend of happiness and tragedy. The same could be said of every case Miss May, Teeny and I had worked together.

Back at the party, everyone cheered as Germany led me onto the dance floor. I looked out at the smiling faces and laughed. *If only things could stay so peaceful in Pine Grove forever*, I thought.

But things were never peaceful for long, even in our quaint small town. I rested my head on Germany's shoulder and hoped at least there'd be a few months, even a year, before I had to deal with any new mysteries.

Germany twirled me under his arm, and as I spun around, my vision capturing blurred visions of my friends, my family, my home, I took solace in knowing that whatever the future held, I could handle it. As long as I was surrounded by love.

Even if there was another murder coming soon...

The End

Dear Reader,

Thank you for reading! I hope you enjoyed this book and liked spending a little time in Pine Grove with Chelsea, Teeny and Miss May.

The next book in this series - *Dread and Butter* -finds our girls investigating yet another murder in Pine Grove.

You'll love this story because it has a mystery that's tough to solve, plus it's got a secret bread recipe that some might even kill for...

Search *Dread and Butter* on Amazon to grab your copy today.

Chelsea

Made in the USA
Columbia, SC
22 July 2020

13989310R00159